Book 1

Runaway Buggy

Bill Moore

Carol Duerksen & Maynard Knepp

Illustrations by Susan Bartel

Started: June 1, 2005
Done: June 3, 2005

WILLOWSPRING DOWNS
HILLSBORO, KANSAS

Runaway Buggy
Book 1 — Jonas Series
Copyright © 1995 by WillowSpring Downs

Second Edition
Third Printing, 1997

Printed in the United States of America

Cover and Story Illustrations by Susan Bartel
Page design & layout by C:PROMPT Creations
Hillsboro, Kansas

This story is a fictional account of an Amish family. Names,
characters, places and incidents are either imaginary or are used
fictitiously, and their resemblance, if any, to real persons, living
or dead, is purely coincidental.

Library of Congress Catalog Number: 95-61742
ISBN 0-9648525-0-0

Contents

Chapter 1
Sixteen

"Jonas! Wake up! Time to chore!"

"Yes, Mom!"

Jonas Bontrager lay awake, thinking. Sixteen. Today he was sixteen.

Through his open window, Jonas heard the motor in the milk-house humming. Dad was out milking already—had been since 5:00 a.m. He'd heard the door slam when Dad left the house half an hour ago.

It isn't just another birthday, he thought to himself. He smiled. Today he'd get his own horse, his own buggy. This weekend, he'd go out with the other Amish young folks. Soon, he'd start dating.

He'd go to Wal-Mart and get some Levi's. He'd never worn jeans before—just homemade baggy barn-door pants. And he'd look at the AM/FM radio/CD players. They seemed so... worldly. Evil. Wrong. *And wonderful!* All at the same time.

But before all of that, he'd fix up his buggy. Lots of bright red reflective tape on the back. Carpet on the inside, on the floor and up the front side. Bright red carpet, he decided. He'd stow a cooler under the seat. All the guys had coolers in their buggies. And a CD player. A lot of the other guys had tape players, but he wanted a CD player. Might as well go all out, he thought.

He would, wouldn't he? His forehead creased under his tousled blond hair. He leaned up on one arm and looked out the window at the quiet Amish farmyard. For 16 years he'd lived here with his family, in a rural Kansas community where things of the world were frowned upon—"conveniences" like electricity, cars, radios, telephones. The Amish religion didn't allow them. And for 16 years he hadn't really cared.

But beginning today, he could make some choices. That's what teenagers did. They bought radios and cars, wore worldly clothes, went to movies—pretty much did what they wanted to. Not that their parents liked it, mind you. But they no longer had a lot to say in the matter.

Jonas's 12-year-old brother, David, stirred beside him in the bed they shared. His other two brothers were asleep in another bed in their upstairs bedroom. They seemed so innocent, lying there asleep; 11-year-old Orie, and Robert, eight. Robert's twin sister, Rebecca, shared a room with 14-year-old Roseanne next door.

Yep, he'd be seeing a lot less of his brothers and sisters now, especially on weekends. No more crowding onto each other's laps to go to church in the family surrey. He grinned. In fact, no more church! Yes! This turning 16 was going to be all right!

Jonas swung his legs out of the bed, picked up his barn-door pants from the floor, and stood up to put them on. He slipped on the light homemade cotton shirt and pulled the suspenders stitched to the pants over his shoulders. Buttoning up the front flap, he began walking across the creaky wooden floor towards the bedroom door. As he walked past Orie and Robert's bed, he tickled their bare feet. Their feet reflexed in response, but the boys ignored the wake-up hint.

"Jonas! Get Up! Your dad's going to be done milking before you get out there!" his mom called again.

"Coming!" Jonas answered. In some ways, his life would be different beginning today. But other things—like the morning chores—wouldn't change at all.

❖ ❖ ❖

Chapter
1

Jonas stepped out of the house into the crisp April morning air, then broke into a sprint to the big red barn across the yard from the house. The family of cats scattered as he braked in front of the door. Jonas laughed, reaching down to pick up a reddish orange tomcat whose motor started immediately.

"Back after a night of visitations, Red?" Jonas asked as he scratched the cat's head. "And now you want your milk. Maybe you should be eating at your girlfriends' houses now and then."

"Morning!" Fred Bontrager greeted his son as he stepped out of the barn and poured milk into the cats' dish. "Your calves are wondering if you forgot about them. Are you sick? Do you need to go back to bed? Maybe you're not up to going to town with me today."

Jonas chuckled at his dad's sense of humor. Sure, there were times when it got old. But mostly, he liked it.

"Guess I do feel a little strange," he rubbed his stomach. "But maybe a trip to Wellsford would help. I think I need about four miles of Kansas wind to fix whatever's ailing me."

"Well, I need to take a load of wheat in after breakfast, so you can come along," his dad replied.

Both Jonas and his father knew the trip to Wellsford had another purpose. But Jonas knew it wasn't appropriate for him to mention it. And Fred? Fred knew that Jonas knew, but he still pretended it was a surprise. That's just the way they did things.

By 7:00 a.m. all of the children were up and had done their assigned morning chores. Standing in the large utility room next to the kitchen, they smelled the breakfast sausage frying as they took off their chore shoes.

"Hurry up, kids, you need to get going to school, and you want to have time to *help Jonas celebrate his birthday*," Esther Bontrager called to her children, laughing as she announced the part about Jonas's birthday. "Quickly now!"

Moments later, eight bowed heads surrounded the table. The long silent grace ended with Fred's audible "Amen!"

"This is the last of the sausage, but I thought this was a good morning to have it," Esther passed the plate of steaming links to Jonas. "Happy birthday."

"Happy birthday to you, happy birthday to you, you look like a monkey, and you act like one too!" the twins sang in unison, arms and hands wildly gyrating in all directions.

"Children!" Fred said sternly. "Eat!"

"Oh, but we'll get him when we're done eating," Orie said. He grinned mischievously.

Jonas had no more than soaked up the syrup on his plate with the last piece of pancake when he felt his chair being pulled away from the table. Roseanne stood behind him, giggling. Taking their cue, the other children grabbed Jonas's legs and arms and began to push him to the floor.

"Under the table, birthday boy, under the table, birthday boy!" they chanted.

Jonas struggled just enough so that all of the kids ended up under the table with him. He didn't know how the family tradition started, but everyone, parents included, had to go under the table on their birthday. The kids always fought it—that was more fun. And sometimes the parents did, too. But the most fun they'd ever had was on their mom's last birthday. She'd said, "If I have to sit under here, you're going to sit here with me, and we're all going to eat here." So there they sat, eating their supper on the floor, beneath the table, when Grandpa and Grandma Yoder's buggy rolled into the driveway. Jonas would never forget how they'd laughed, and how Grandpa Yoder joked, "Esther always was the strangest one of my children."

"It's almost 8:00!" Rebecca shrieked, jumping up from where she was sitting on Jonas's leg under the table. "Rowdy'll have to run like crazy to get us to school on time!"

Robert, Orie, and David followed close on their sister's heels as she flew out the door. Rowdy, their Shetland pony, stood waiting at the hitching post, a small two-seated wagon behind him. The four youngest Bontrager children piled into the wagon, David slapped the reins across Rowdy's back, and they headed out the driveway. Jonas, Roseanne, and their parents watched from the door, Esther's "Not so fast!!" lost in the clatter as the wagon careened around the corner and onto the sand road.

Like all Amish children, Jonas and Roseanne's formal education ended with the eighth grade. The Amish community didn't believe "higher education" was necessary—or good—for their children. Too many worldly influences entered their lives in high school. A basic knowledge of reading, writing, and arithmetic

was all they needed from school. The rest of their "life skills" they'd learn at home and from life itself.

Jonas turned from the doorway. "I'll get ready to go," he told his father as he strode toward the stairway. Taking the steps two at a time, he almost felt like letting out a whoop. This morning he was getting his very own brand-new buggy!

Fred Bontrager was hitching up the mule team to the wagonload of wheat when Jonas showed up in his "town" clothes—barn-door pants and a cotton shirt very similar to the ones he'd had on, only newer. He helped his dad finish hitching the team. Then they climbed onto the tall springboard seat.

"Let's go, Belle. C'mon, Burt!" Fred slapped the reins across the broad backs of the two mules. The wagon began creaking its way down the drive, and turned onto the road to Wellsford.

Jonas tried to act like it was just another trip into Wellsford, but his blue eyes shone with anticipation. He sat in silence for most of the forty-minute drive into town, thinking about the changes in his life beginning today, and listening to the meadowlarks singing on the high-line wires above the road. It was one of those perfect spring mornings—the kind when a person almost felt sorry for the people trapped in their fast cars and hurried lives as they whizzed past the mule-drawn wagon. *They sure can't enjoy the morning like we can,* Jonas thought to himself.

The patron-owned Co-op grain elevator, located on the edge of Wellsford, did a thriving business with the Amish community. At the Co-op driveway, Fred stopped the mules as a large semi-truck full of grain turned in front of them onto the elevator lot, then signaled them to follow. After the truck had weighed its load on the concrete slab, Fred guided the team onto the scale. That done, it was time for them to unload the wheat in the huge white elevator building.

Now as far as the mules were concerned, pulling a load of wheat for four miles in a wooden-wheeled wagon was no big deal.

Standing behind a noisy, smelly diesel truck could be tolerated. But walking into a monstrous tall but scary, narrow building that was making loud noises? That's where they put their hooves down.

And they did. They stood, black bodies and hooves planted firmly at the elevator opening, their ears stubbornly thrown back in a defiant slant.

"Burt! Belle! Git, you stupid mules!" Fred commanded, slapping the reins hard. "C'mon! Get in there!"

But the team stood its ground, and no amount of coercive yelling and rein-slapping made any difference. To make matters worse, another farmer had pulled up behind the Bontrager wagon, waiting to unload his wheat.

"Turn them out and let the guy behind us go," Jonas said. "Do we have any grain with us?"

"Half-ass mules," Fred muttered. "What good is that going to do?"

Before Jonas could answer, Fred had signaled the team to turn sharply to the right. Thinking they'd won, they readily obeyed, and the team and wagon rumbled away from the awesome elevator doors.

"No, we don't have any grain other than the wheat," Fred answered his son. "You think you can tempt them in?"

"It's worth a try, isn't it?"

Jonas jumped down from the wagon and ran into the elevator building. He returned soon with a bucket of horse feed. Standing in front of the long-eared pair, he took turns feeding them from the bucket. After a few minutes, he put the bucket over his arm and took a mule's bridle in each hand.

"C'mon, Burt. Belle, let's go." The team followed Jonas dutifully as he led them back around and once again to the elevator entrance. Then they stopped.

Jonas turned to face the mules. "Okay, here's the deal," he

explained to the broad faces regarding him with benign, resolute stares. "You love grain. I have grain. Here's some now." He paused, and gave them each another mouthful. "And now you'll have to come get it," he said, and stepped inside the elevator.

The mules never did trust that monster building with its loud grain-drying fans, and their ears flicked nervously back and forth, back and forth. But they did love their grain, and finally the temptation was too great. Reluctantly, they followed Jonas into the building, inch by daring inch, and the Bontrager wheat was unloaded without any more major problems.

Jonas stayed with the team while Fred went into the office to get his check for the wheat. When he climbed back up onto the wagon seat, Fred inquired nonchalantly, "Any other business you have in town?" His laughing eyes told Jonas he didn't expect an answer as he turned the team towards downtown Wellsford.

Miller's Buggy Shop stood in the middle of Wellsford, and a thriving business it was. Leon Miller built and repaired buggies not only for the Amish community, but for a wide variety of people who used horses and buggies for recreation. Some people said he was too expensive—that he was catering too much to the "outside" market. But there wasn't much they could do about it. Unless they ordered a buggy from out of state and had it transported in, they did business with Miller's.

Jonas jumped down from the wagon and tied Belle and Burt at Miller's hitching post, then walked into the shop with his father.

"Hello, Fred. Jonas," Leon greeted the pair. "What can I do for you today?"

"Jonas here thinks he needs a buggy," Fred said and winked. "Got anything used that won't fall apart if he has a runaway?"

"I'm sure we can fix him up," Leon said. "I think we got a trade-in just the other day."

Jonas's heart sank. He knew they'd come to town to get him

a buggy. But…well, he'd figured it'd be a *new* one. All of the other guys got new buggies when they turned 16. What had he done that he didn't deserve a new one? Or couldn't his parents afford it? Either way, he was really disappointed. But he'd never show it.

"'Course you know what I mean by 'used,' don't you, Leon?" Fred's voice broke into Jonas's thoughts as they walked outside to the row of buggies and surreys. "One that your children played in while you were making it. Figure that's worth a small discount, don't you?"

Leon and Jonas both realized at the same time that Fred had been joking—as usual.

"Ah yes, we have lots of that kind." Jonas thought Leon sounded about as relieved as Jonas felt. They were looking at a new buggy after all! "Let's take a gander at these over here."

Jonas's eyes swept down the line of identical-appearing black wooden boxes. It seemed the only difference was that some were single-seated buggies and others two-seated surreys.

"Got one spotted?" Leon asked.

"Guess the single buggies are all about the same."

"Yeah, except this one." Leon walked over to the buggy at the end of the row. "Just finished this one yesterday. Built it for a young guy. Put red carpet on the floor. You're the first one to look at it."

As they drove to their farm, Jonas kept glancing back at the new buggy rolling along behind the wagon. Amish weren't supposed to be proud of anything, but he couldn't help but beam at the shiny black body, the beautiful blue upholstered seat, and the bright red carpet. Add some reflective tape on the back in fun designs, and a good-looking, fast horse—yes, he'd have quite the rig.

"The girls will be standing in line to get a ride in your new buggy," Jonas's dad said, glancing sideways at the youth who'd seemed to grow from a toddler to manhood overnight. "You know how to handle girls?"

For once, Jonas didn't know if his father was joking or serious. And he couldn't tell from the deadpan expression on his face either.

"Well, I guess I'll learn," Jonas answered. "Any tips?" He cleared his throat nervously, hoping to keep his voice from cracking.

His father was silent for a while before he finally said, "Don't date girls who drink or smoke—and you and I both know full well some of the Amish do. Don't date English girls, either, because what happens if you fall in love? If you'd end up marrying outside the Amish and leave, it would break my heart. Your mother's, too."

Jonas had never heard his father sound so serious in all his life. Neither did he have any idea at that moment how many times those words would come back to play over and over again in his mind.

Chapter 2

Price to Pay

While Fred and Jonas were in town, Esther and Roseanne Bontrager had been busy cleaning the house in preparation for a surprise birthday party that evening. Roseanne had also baked Jonas's favorite dessert, Mississippi Mud Cake, for lunch that day. Jonas had just polished off his second piece of cake when he heard a horse and buggy approaching their lane. He glanced out the window in time to see a dark brown, sweat-lathered horse take the corner at a run and pull up to the hitching post, snorting and stomping his hooves. A tall boy, about Jonas's age, jumped out of the open hack buggy and tied up his horse.

"It's Enos Lee," Jonas said, heading out the door to meet him.

"Hey!" Enos greeted Jonas, his dark eyes laughing from under a broad-brimmed straw hat. "Heard you were in town this morning. Heard you got some new wheels!"

"Yeah. How'd you know?"

"Stopped by the buggy shop. Leon told me."

"Wanna see it?"

"Well, I didn't come here just to say 'Happy Birthday!'" Enos pointed out and shoved Jonas playfully. "You need an expert to help you wire it, don't you?"

Thirty minutes later, Jonas approached his father. "Dad, Enos and I thought we'd run into Wellsford and get some stuff for the buggy," he said.

Fred looked up from the horse-drawn mower he was repairing. "I kinda thought you'd be giving me a hand here this afternoon," he grunted as he tried to loosen a bolt. "Besides, we just got back from Wellsford this morning."

The teenagers exchanged glances, and Enos's dark eyes clouded. Jonas rarely argued with his father. But he really wanted to get his buggy rigged up, especially with Enos there to help. Enos knew what to do. He'd done it before.

"I know, Dad. It's just that Enos had some time today to help me," Jonas said, his head down, his right tennis shoe tracing a circle in the sand. "Can't David help you?"

Fred seemed to be concentrating extra hard on a bolt he was unscrewing. Jonas knew his dad was thinking, and all he could do was wait.

Finally Fred looked up from the mower. "Tell your mom to give you $20," he said. "Tell her it's your birthday money, and you're going to town to buy lights and tape for your buggy. And I'll expect a *lot* of work out of you tomorrow."

"You bet, Dad!" Jonas said, slapping Enos on the shoulder. "Let's go!"

The trip into town with Enos Lee's fast horse and light open buggy was much quicker than the one Jonas had taken that morning with his father. The boys' conversation about what it meant to run around with the young folks also made the time fly. A year older than Jonas, Enos had a lot of stories to tell, and his 16-year-old friend was all ears.

"Look, Elton's here," Enos said as he pulled up next to a horse tied at the hardware store's hitching rack. "Probably came in to get supplies. He's working on that carpenter crew, you know."

Then why'd he ride in, rather than driving the crew's pickup? Jonas wondered. He loves to tear around in that truck.

Jonas knew that allowing Amish men to drive vehicles for business purposes was one of the concessions the community had started making in the last few years. The vehicles were owned by businesses for which the Amish men worked, and the guys used them to run errands and even to commute back and forth from work. Although owning and driving a car was forbidden by the Amish religion, the rules got bent a little in certain cases. Especially if the driver was a young man who hadn't yet joined the church. Elton fit that category.

"Hey, Jonas, Enos Lee. What's happening?" Elton was just walking out the door as the two boys got there.

"Came to get lights and red tape for his buggy," Enos nudged his friend. "Jonas's 16 today."

"Oh!" Elton nodded knowingly. "You'll be needing a tape player for that buggy too, I bet."

"Yeah. Actually, I was thinking I'd get a CD player," Jonas said.

"I'll make you one heck of a deal," Elton said, lingering. He could smell a sale. "I'm going to be joining church. I've got a few things to get rid of, including my stereo/cassette player. Works great. Sell it to you for a $20 bill. You can't touch a CD player for that."

"So that's why you're riding instead of burning rubber in that pickup?" Enos laughed. "Joining church, huh? Don't 'spose Vera would be joining at about the same time, would she?"

Elton blushed at the hint that he and his steady girlfriend were joining in order to get married, even though everyone knew it was the case. He turned to Jonas. "It's in my buggy at home. You can stop by there on your way home and take it. What d'ya think?"

Jonas didn't know what he thought. Sure he wanted something—stereo, tape or CD player in his buggy. But this was all so quick. And it would mean using the money from his parents. Buying a stereo was bad enough. Buying it with their money was like a stab in the back.

"Stop by and listen to it. I'll even throw in the tapes. If you want it, leave the money in the buggy," Elton said. "I've gotta go. The guys are waiting for these nails."

"Can't beat that deal." Enos looked at Jonas as Elton jumped on his horse and kicked it into a gallop.

"I don't know. If I buy it, I won't have money for the wiring and lights and red tape. And I've got to have that first."

"Tell you what. I'll loan you the cash for the other stuff. You've gotta buy it, man."

"Dad'll be really ticked off," Jonas argued. "Why... he'll... and Mama will..."

"Oh, *excuse* me! I must have the wrong Jonas Bontrager! The one *I* know turned 16 today. He's not going to be asking his Mommy and Daddy for permission for everything he does from now on!"

Jonas recoiled at the dripping sarcasm from Enos. But Enos was right.

"Yeah. Okay. Let's at least take a look at it."

It was late afternoon when the boys got back to Jonas's home, and they quickly got to work on the buggy.

"Looks like you'll be ready for Saturday night," the voice caught the teenagers by surprise. Engrossed in their work, they hadn't heard or seen Fred walk up. Jonas's eyes automatically fell on the stereo lying on the seat, and his father's eyes followed the path of his glance.

"Yeah, now all he needs is a girl," Enos Lee joked. But Jonas wasn't smiling, and Fred seemed preoccupied with other thoughts as well.

"Oh, I'm sure he'll get that, too," Fred said as he walked away, a tired slump to his shoulders.

The lightheartedness was gone from his voice and Jonas hurt to know his father was disappointed with him. He hadn't said a word about the stereo. He didn't have to.

Every time they passed each other while doing the evening

chores, Jonas expected his father to ask about the stereo, but he didn't. Fred usually whistled while he milked the cows. This evening, the only sound in the dairy parlor was the whoosh-whoosh of the automatic milker. Jonas found himself wishing for a scolding—anything would be better than this silence. He'll probably bring it up in front of the whole family during supper, Jonas thought.

"Jonas, meet me in the horse barn when you're done with your chores," Fred finally broke the stillness.

Jonas flinched inwardly. Surely he was too old for a whipping. It'd been a long time since his dad had laid a hand on him. But then, he hadn't done anything to deserve it. He'd been a good, obedient kid. Until today.

Fred was feeding the horses in their stalls when Jonas trudged slowly into the barn. Ever since he was old enough to walk, Jonas had loved the faded red barn. It always promised fun and surprises for children—kittens and chicken nests hiding in the straw, a ladder up into the hayloft, secret hiding places, a rope swing. Decades of housing horses and storing hay gave the barn a distinct aroma—a sweet pungent smell of which Jonas never tired.

"I figured you'd get a stereo sometime," Fred said quietly, forking hay into the manger. "But today? With the money we gave you? Why?"

"Elton was getting rid of it—cheap," Jonas hung his head.

"I see. Well, I'm disappointed. But it's done," Fred paused. "That buggy of yours isn't much good without a horse," he continued as Jonas began scratching the neck of the dark brown horse in the first stall. The gelding moved his big body towards Jonas's hand, eating up the attention without missing a bite of his grain. "Have you been thinking about which horse you want?"

Of course he had. He just couldn't believe his dad wanted to talk about that now.

"Well, yeah. I've always liked Lightning, you know."

"You saw him soon after he was born. And you named him, didn't you?"

"Yeah, his white blaze kinda reminded me of a lightning bolt. And I guess I was hoping he'd be as fast as lightning."

"You heard what Irvin said when he broke him. He *is* fast. Still a bit spooky, though. He's young." Fred paused. "But he's yours, if you want him."

Jonas looked at his dad, a wide smile spreading across his face. "I do. Thanks, Dad. Thanks a lot!"

When Fred and Jonas walked out of the barn, they noticed a horse and buggy tied up at the hitching post.

"It's Grandpa and Grandma Yoder," Jonas said. "Wonder what they want?"

"Who knows?"

"Are they here for supper?"

"And what makes you think that?" Fred Bontrager asked, with studied innocence.

"Just a wild idea," Jonas laughed, breaking into a run for the house, as his father increased his own gait.

By the time Jonas and Fred had showered, the house smelled of frying hamburgers, and relatives were walking in every few minutes. Jonas's mother, Esther, had six brothers and sisters, each with at least four children. A quick inventory by Jonas confirmed what he'd suspected—they were all present for his birthday.

"So, Jonas, what did you get for your birthday?" his 15-year-old cousin Lyndon asked.

"He got a new buggy!" Jonas's brother Robert yelled.

"It has red carpet. And a ster—" A quick hand clamped over Robert's mouth stopped him mid-word.

"You little snoop!" Jonas hissed, and quickly took his hand away from Robert's mouth. "One more word, and I'll take you out

**Chapter
2**

to the barn and paddle you myself," he promised, and lightning flashed across his normally serene eyes. Robert squirmed away and ran off to join his cousins. Lyndon grinned at Jonas. "Maybe after supper we can go out and *listen* to this new *buggy* of yours," he said under his breath.

Supper was the usual combination of good food, jokes, talking about people and events in the community, and catching up with each other's lives.

When it was time for dessert, Esther caught the eyes of several of her sisters, and they began singing "Happy Birthday." Everyone else joined in while Jonas smiled and flushed with embarrassment at being the center of attention.

"Six-six-sixteen and never been kissed. Saturday night you'll find out what you've missed!" the chant arose from several of Jonas's young cousins as soon as the traditional song was over.

"So, Jonas, who'll be the lucky girl to *schnitzel* you?" his youngest uncle teased as he helped himself to a big bowl of homemade ice cream. "If you're lucky like me, you'll end up marrying her!" he winked at his pretty wife. "Then again, you've got lots of girls to check out before you think about marryin' one, eh?"

Jonas blushed at the reference to being "schnitzeled." Tradition among the Amish teens called for a girl who was already with the young folks to introduce a boy who'd just turned 16 to the rudiments of "making out." This kissing episode was more a rite of passage than the result of passion, and "who schnitzeled whom" was a great topic of conversation.

"I hear he has one hot buggy—red carpet and everything," Lyndon noted. "The girls will be standing in line."

"Six-six-sixteen and never been kissed," the chant began again.

Seeing her son's face redden with each remark, Esther decided to come to his rescue. "I think it's time for presents," she said.

Like the gift of a horse and buggy from his parents, the other presents Jonas got for his 16th birthday symbolized his passage from childhood into young adulthood. One of his aunts had made him a shirt. Unlike the plain shirts he'd been wearing up until now, this one sported the yoke styling of a western shirt, and a pocket. Pockets were illegal for boys under 16 and for men who had joined the church. But Jonas was in-between. He was now a "simmy."

Among the Amish young people, a "simmy" was a boy who had just turned 16 and was starting to run around. Still somewhat innocent but learning the ropes fast, simmies suffered from the same kind of harassment their "worldly" counterparts did as freshmen in high school. The best part about being a simmy was being old enough to be one, and then being old enough *not* to be one anymore.

"A simmy needs his own flashlight." Jonas's Uncle Ben kidded as Jonas opened a gift and held it up for the family to see. "Just don't go any place, or do anything I wouldn't do, with that flashlight."

"Yeah, right," Jonas responded, as the family exchanged knowing glances. Ben had been a real terror as a teenager. And, as often happened, he was now a deacon in the church.

As he opened the last gift, Jonas's mouth fell open, and he looked around at the room full of relatives.

"Who is this from?"

"We picked it up at the Shipshewana Flea Market when we were in Indiana," Grandpa answered. "A boy with his own horse and buggy should have one."

Jonas lifted the heavy fur lap robe up for everyone to see, and the room was filled with oohs and ahhhs.

"Can I touch it?" a three-year-old cousin begged.

"Sure, come see how soft it is. Here, feel it here. Grandpa, is this *real*?"

"Real as the naked buffalo who gave it up," Grandpa teased. "The guy I bought it from raises buffalo. He has them butchered, sells the meat, tans the hides and sells them. It should last a long time. Someday, you can give it to your grandson."

Jonas scanned the room full of people. He loved his family— their humor, their deep caring for each other, their unity in faith and tradition, the belonging and security he felt among them.

Turning 16 would mean spending weekends with the young folks, and missing many of these family get-togethers. Guess that's the price you pay, he thought, surprised at the odd sense of sadness mingling with elation in his heart.

Chapter 3
First Weekend Out

When Enos Lee careened his horse and buggy into the Bontrager driveway early Saturday evening, Jonas threw a quick good-bye at whoever might hear it, and bounded out the door. He'd donned his best barn-door pants—other than his church ones, of course—and his new western shirt. Enos, he noticed right away, had on Levi's.

"Ready for your first wild and crazy night out on the town?" Enos grinned down at Jonas from the buggy seat. "Let's go chase some girls!"

"Yeah, right," Jonas climbed onto the seat. "It's just that easy, huh?"

"Sure! Sometimes *they* even chase *you*, especially those English girls. Could be one of them will have the hots for you, and ask *you* out."

Could be, Jonas thought to himself as they headed out the lane and Enos set his horse in a fast trot towards Wellsford. But probably not. Enos seemed so confident and self-assured about everything. Jonas didn't.

For years, one of the regular meeting places for the Amish young people was the Star Bowl bowling alley in Wellsford. They brought a lot of business into the place, and the hitching rack on the back side of the building was almost as old as Star Bowl itself. Jonas and Enos Lee's fathers had tied their horses up at that rack two decades earlier; tonight Enos pulled his horse up to the half dozen horses and buggies already there. More would be coming, others leaving as the evening progressed.

The sounds of balls rolling down the lanes, pins falling, and a juke box spouting out an old Elvis tune greeted Jonas's ears as he and Enos stepped into the bowling alley. A small group of Amish youth was hanging out in one corner near a pool table.

Chapter 3

"Hey, wanna shoot some pool?" one of them called. "Jonas! I'll teach you how to play. See this black ball? You want to get him in a pocket as fast as you can!"

"Don't trust him," another one warned, sighting a ball with the cue stick. "Dave promised to teach me how to handle a beer or two, and I *still* can't remember the lesson!"

Everyone laughed, including Dave. Dave grinned at Jonas. "After this game is over, I'll show you the ropes. Nothing to it. Just practice and a little luck."

By 9:00 p.m., Dave and some of the other older guys had left the bowling alley to find more action elsewhere. Jonas, Enos, and two other boys had a pool tournament going, and weren't paying a lot of attention to the people coming and going around them.

"Never seen *him* before," Jonas heard young feminine voices. "He's kinda cute...nice butt in those funny pants."

Jonas looked around to see who was talking, and his eyes met three non-Amish girls about his age, watching him from the next pool table. Jonas's face turned pink beneath their teasing gazes.

"He's kinda shy. It's his first weekend out." Enos entered the one-way conversation to explain. "Jonas, this is Debbie, Tara, and Alison," he gestured in the general direction of the girls. "They hang out here a lot, too. And they think going for a buggy ride with a good-looking Amish dude is too cool for words."

"Enos knows how to have fun in a buggy," Debbie, the one who'd been talking about Jonas, giggled. "How about you?"

Jonas would have given anything to be in a buggy at that moment, alone, driving home. Why did they have to notice him

22

tonight? His first night out? What should he say? He had to say something.

"I don't have my buggy here tonight," he met Debbie's laughing green eyes. Cute, he thought, noting her impish smile, little upturned nose and wavy blond hair. "But when I do, if you still want a ride, I'll give you one."

When Star Bowl closed at midnight, the four Amish boys and their English friends were still playing pool and talking.

"So, where are you girls going now?" Enos asked, his eyes on the petite brunette named Tara.

"Oh, we have to go home. We have 12 o'clock curfews. Stupid, huh," Tara answered, returning Enos's look. "Don't you guys have curfews?"

"Curfews? What do you mean, 'curfews'?"

"A time when your parents make you be at home."

Enos let out a guffaw. "I have to be home in time to go to work Monday morning!"

"But this is Saturday night! Aren't you home between now and then?"

"Doubt it!" Enos grinned mischievously. "I'm sure we'll find better things to do."

Jonas glanced at his friend, and then at the girls. They were obviously surprised that these teenagers from the ultra-conservative Amish had fewer restrictions than they did. He didn't understand it all himself. But he was learning. Boy was he learning!

Knowing that the Amish girls were having a party at Sue Ann Eash's home, the guys headed over there from the bowling alley. The dark farmyard hummed with activity and the glowing light of Coleman lanterns scattered around the yard. Music from a boom box drifted through the cool, still night air, and Jonas could see kids playing cards, talking, eating and drinking.

"We were wondering if you'd end up over here," Sue Ann greeted the guys. "We heard you were over at Star Bowl, flirting

with the girls there. How's your first night out, Jonas?"

"Great!" he said, taking in the young woman standing in the circle of light from the lantern she carried. Sue Ann was two years older. Until now, he'd always seen her with her dark brown hair confined under a white Amish covering, but tonight it was flowing down her back in waves of beguiling softness. Her high cheek bones, dancing dark eyes, and flashing white smile made her one of the prettiest of the Amish girls, Jonas decided. And she was wearing tight jeans. Jeans and a white Garth Brooks T-shirt.

Chapter
3

"Did you go to his concert?" Jonas asked, nodding at the T-shirt.

"You know it! Sam stood in line all night to get tickets, and it was worth every minute of it. You like Garth?"

"Yeah, but I haven't heard him much. Guess I'll have to buy some of his tapes."

"Oh, you can borrow mine. I don't mind," she said as a tall good-looking guy came up and put his arm around her waist. "Well, I've gotta go. Sam and I promised Robert and Ruth we'd play a round of cards with them."

Sometime around 3:00 a.m. the party started winding down. Couples were leaving in buggies or slipping quietly into the house. Sam and Sue Ann had retreated to his bright red Camero to "listen to tapes," as they explained when they left the card players. Jonas envied Sam. A hot car and the best-looking girl around—what more could a guy want?

"You ever gonna get a car?" Jonas asked Enos as they left the farmyard.

"I've thought about it. Folks would have a fit, but I don't really care. What can they do anyway?"

"I've heard Sam's dad was so mad at him, he wouldn't talk to him for a week. And then when he did, it was a sermon about how he was going to drive himself right into hell. And his dad said that since he's responsible for his children staying in the church, God is holding him accountable for what Sam does. He really laid it on Sam."

"Yeah, well, we get that in church too, you know," Enos said. After a long pause, he asked, "Do you really think Sam is going to hell because he has a car?"

"I don't know. The preachers sure talk a lot about how wide the road is to destruction, and how narrow the road is to heaven. I'd think an Amish guy driving a car would be on the wide road."

"But what about all of the other people who drive cars? And what about the Amish guys who have a car until they join the church?"

Jonas didn't answer. Enos was asking the same questions he was beginning to have himself, and there didn't seem to be any answers. For long moments both boys were lost in their own thoughts, until Enos finally chuckled softly and said, "Guess I could buy one and see what happens."

Jonas didn't laugh.

Hours later, Jonas, Enos, and two other guys without dates crashed at Enos's house, despite Enos's earlier prediction that he probably wouldn't go home all weekend. They still needed a place to sleep and grab some food. It seemed the four had barely fallen across the saggy double bed mattress when Jonas awoke to hear Enos's father calling his sons to get up. Enos's brothers in the other bed responded dutifully, and left to help with the morning chores. Enos didn't even bother to answer—his dad didn't expect him to.

Listening to the sounds of a family rising and going outside, Jonas knew his family was several miles away doing the same thing. They'd come in, eat a quick breakfast, and then leave for church, he mused. Church was at the Miller family farm just down the road, so they wouldn't have far to go. They might even walk, if it was a nice morning. Mom would probably wonder out loud where he was, and say she missed him being with the family. He didn't really miss them, but he felt weird sleeping in on Sunday morning, and in a strange bed with three other guys. He was so tired.

Around noon, the guys got up and made hot dogs for themselves, then spent the afternoon back at Star Bowl. By supper time they, along with thirty-some other Amish young folks, showed up at the farm of the Miller family who'd hosted church that morning. When a family had church at their home, it meant a morning worship service and noon meal for everyone, then a Sunday evening meal and *singing* for just the young folks.

For the teenagers, a *singing* meant a big meal, socializing, singing traditional Amish religious choruses together, and walking the fine line between pleasing their elders (who were happy to see them there) and being more than a little rebellious. It was always interesting to see if someone would cross that line at a singing.

A beat-up little brown Honda roared onto the Miller yard where the young folks were gathering, and bumped to a stop inches away from the barn. Sam's older brother Sol stepped out, paused, then began weaving his way towards the house.

"This where the singing's at?" he asked of no one in particular. "And some food?"

The other kids looked at each other, half-embarrassed, half-amused. Sol was on a weekend drunk, which wasn't anything new. He could be downright funny when he was trashed. But it wasn't cool for him to show up like this at a singing.

Sam emerged from the crowd where he'd been standing with Sue Ann, and strode towards his brother.

"Let's go in the house," Sam took Sol's elbow and guided him towards the door.

When Sam came back out, the other young folks were gathering near the front door. "I think he'll stay there at the table," he said to Sue Ann, who'd come up to join him. "I gave him a strong cup of coffee to sip while he waits to eat."

Two by two, the teens paired off and filed into the house. Some of them were established couples, going steady, but most of them weren't. The tradition at singings called for the guys, beginning with the oldest, to pick a girl to sit with for the evening. Jonas's eyes followed Sam and Sue Ann into the house, then he turned his attention to the girls left for him to choose from.

The joys of being a simmy, he thought to himself when he saw the three girls still standing outside. I get to choose between the one who hardly ever says a word, the one who's 22 going on 42, and the one who looks like she's eaten too many church cookies.

He nodded at Alma, the shy girl, and they walked in to join the rest of the teens seated on benches at long tables.

After the traditional singing meal of sandwiches, chips, and pie, Sol and a few other guys excused themselves. "Be right back," they said, laughing as they noisily pushed their benches away from the table. "Gotta go behind the barn."

The tables were quickly cleared, and songbooks handed out. One of the older, more responsible fellows started a song, and gradually the rest of the group joined him.

Several songs later, the singers heard loud voices outside the house. Making no move to go in, Sol and his buddies stood outside, telling jokes and laughing. Sitting near the open window, Jonas could hear a lot of what they said. He chuckled to himself at the off-color jokes. They were certainly more interesting than the songs he'd been singing!

"They're not funny," Linda, the 22-going-on-42 year-old sitting across the table from him, said. "Guys like that give us a bad name. People think Amish kids are all wild and crazy."

"Ah, Linda, lighten up," Jonas heard himself saying. "All Amish kids aren't any more like them than they are like you. They're just having a little fun."

"I wouldn't call showing up drunk and telling dirty jokes at a singing just a little fun," she retorted. "You're just a simmy, and if you're approving of those guys' behavior, you're headed in the wrong direction early."

Yeah, and you're headed straight for old-maid-hood, he thought but didn't say out loud. Linda had probably joined the church the minute she turned 16—her family always did act like they were a little better than everyone else.

"You gonna drive your own horse and buggy next weekend?" Enos asked Jonas on the way home.

"Probably. I still need to put the red tape on the back, but I'll do that this week."

"Unless, of course, you want a ride in a car," Enos hinted.

"Whose car?"

"Mine."

"You getting a car?"

"Sol wants to sell his Honda and get something better."

"You gonna buy that piece of junk?"

"It's cheap, and it runs."

"You really going to get a car?" Jonas repeated.

"You think there's something wrong with that?"

"Well, no. I don't know," Jonas paused before continuing. "Guess I'll drive myself though. I'd like to try out the new buggy, and see how Lightning drives."

"Suit yourself," Enos said, and Jonas felt just a touch of disappointment and frustration in his voice. For all of Jonas's bravado in front of Linda about loosening up her expectations of the young folks, he couldn't get used to the idea of Enos buying Sol's car. He didn't like it. But he didn't know why.

Chapter 4

Debbie

Several weeks after his birthday, Jonas was getting used to the new routine. During the week, he stayed home and helped with the farm work. But from Saturday evening until sometime in the early morning hours of Monday, he was gone. Out with the young folks.

"Must be Monday morning. Jonas looks like he hasn't slept for days," Fred half-joked at the breakfast table one rainy morning in mid-May.

"He's with the girls; he doesn't have time to sleep," David chimed in. "Who was it this weekend, Jonas? And what's that funny mark on your neck?"

"I think you're looking at a man who's been schnitzeled," Roseanne giggled. "Either that, or he needs to go to the doctor for a very serious spider bite."

Almost too tired to react to the teasing, Jonas put another spoonful of cereal in his mouth and simultaneously kicked his sister under the table.

"Ow!" Roseanne shrieked.

"I think the problem is he needs more work to fill his time," Fred continued. "He needs a job—somebody that expects him to be there bright and early on Monday morning. What do you think, Jonas?"

What did he think? What *could* he think? If his dad thought he should get a job, he'd get a job. He was old enough to help support the family, whatever that took. Whether he stayed home and worked for nothing, or got a job in the community, the money from his labor would go to his father. That's just the way it was.

"You know somebody who would hire me?" Jonas lifted the cereal bowl to his mouth and drank the last of the milk.

"I hear Harlan Schmidt, the big dairyman north of Wellsford, could use a hired hand. Thought maybe we'd go talk to him today, since it's rainin' and we can't do much around here anyway."

So it happened that the next morning, Jonas found himself milking cows at one of the biggest dairies in the community. Harlan's wife had picked Jonas up at 5:00, saving him the hour-long trip in his buggy. He'd felt strange riding in a car with a woman he'd never met before, but he figured he'd get used to it.

Jonas had just let the last of the cows out of the milk barn when he noticed a girl about his age, not far away, feeding the newborn calves with a bucket of milk. Her head was bent down and her back turned to him, but somehow she looked familiar. Where had he seen her before?

Just then, she pulled the bucket away from the calf and turned to move on to the next one. She glanced up and met Jonas's surprised stare with one of her own.

"You're...um, I don't remember your name," she said, blushing. "You're one of those Amish guys that was at the Star Bowl a few weeks ago."

"Yeah, you're Debbie. I remember you." The cute one, he thought to himself. The same intriguing green eyes that had laughed at him at the Star Bowl smiled at him now. "You live here?" he asked.

Debbie laughed, and Jonas realized how stupid the question must've sounded.

"No, I just come here at the crack of dawn to feed somebody else's stupid calves," she answered lightly, and giggled again. Walking to the next calf that was bawling for its milk, she said "Yeah, I live here. What are *you* doing here?"

"Well, I guess I do get up at the crack of dawn to milk somebody else's stupid cows," Jonas chuckled. "I started working for your dad today."

"Really? Cool!" she paused. "Look, would you mind finishing up these last few calves? I'm running late and I've gotta get ready for school. Thanks! See ya!"

Before Jonas could say anything, Debbie was running for the house, and all he could hear was the bawling of the hungry baby calves.

So Harlan Schmidt is Debbie's father, he thought. Now this could be interesting.

Harlan took Jonas home that evening after chores, and they were barely out of the driveway when he let Jonas know how pleased he was with him.

"You're a good worker, and I'm glad to have you as a hired hand," Harlan complimented the teenager. "I know that all the money you make has to go to your father, but if you keep up the good work, I'm willing to make a deal with you. I'll give you a calf every now and then. If it's a bull calf, you can sell it for the cash. If it's a heifer calf, you can keep it to start your own herd someday. They can stay here, and your dad doesn't ever have to know about it. Sound okay to you?"

Jonas could hardly believe his ears. Sound okay? All he had to do was work hard and be responsible, which he was used to doing anyway, and Harlan would give him that kind of a bonus?

"Sounds great!" he grinned broadly. "You really mean it?"

"Of course I do. And there's one other thing. I'm wondering if you could get your driver's license so we don't always have to pick you up and take you home? I know Amish guys sometimes drive to and from work if somebody gives them a vehicle to drive. We've got an old pickup you could use."

This news wasn't so good. Jonas was quiet awhile before answering.

"I don't know. I'll ask my dad. But I don't think he's going to let me do that."

"You talk to him. Tell him it's important if you're going to keep this job. Tell him I remember him driving when he was about your age. See what he says to that."

Armed with Harlan's logic, Jonas hoped for the best when he broached the topic with his father right before bedtime.

"No. The answer is no," Fred Bontrager stated flatly.

"Harlan said I need my license if I'm going to work for him."

"You work one day and he's already telling you to drive?"

"They don't have time to pick me up and bring me home every day," Jonas argued.

"Then you can take your horse and buggy, or just ride Lightning over there."

"But that's an hour…"

"It won't hurt you."

"Harlan said you drove when you were my age." Jonas was almost surprised to hear himself arguing with his dad. But he wanted this job.

"What I did when I was your age is really none of Harlan's business, nor yours," Fred's voice was hard. "Harlan wasn't exactly the perfect guy himself, but that's not the point. The point is, you're not going to get your driver's license. If you're worth so much to them, they can pick you up."

Harlan didn't bring up the driver's license again, and Jonas certainly wasn't going to. The rest of the week passed uneventfully. Jonas enjoyed milking at the large modern dairy, and seeing Debbie during chore time wasn't half bad either.

"So, what are you guys doing this weekend?" Debbie asked casually while they were finishing up with the calves late Friday afternoon. Jonas had started regularly helping her with the bucket calves if he was done with his job before she was finished.

"Oh, the usual. There'll be a party somewhere, I guess."

"Really? An Amish party? I wonder what they're like. You know, Jonas, you promised me a buggy ride sometime. Remember, at the Star Bowl?"

"Yeah, I remember."

"Well, how about if you and what's his name—Enos?—meet me and Tara at the Star Bowl tomorrow evening? Then you guys could take us to the party. It wouldn't be a date or anything. We just want a fast buggy ride, and to see what happens at an Amish party." The more she said, the faster Debbie talked. And her eyes danced with fun and mischief.

"Oh, I don't know. Enos might not..."

"You ask him. We'll be there tomorrow night. If you decide you don't want to, we'll just figure you think you're too good for us," she said it lightly, but the subtle threat wasn't lost on Jonas.

Although the teasing teenager didn't know it, Debbie had hit a particularly vulnerable spot in Jonas. Part of being Amish meant never being or acting proud. Humility was almost like the 11th commandment. As dedicated as they were to their peculiar beliefs and humble lifestyle, the Amish would never want it said of them that they were "too good" to associate with other people.

Against Jonas's better judgment, he found himself in his buggy with Enos, Debbie and Tara the next evening, leaving the Star Bowl at a fast trot as the Kansas sun went down behind them. His single-seated buggy just had room for two, so the giggling girls were perched on the guys' laps.

"Oh, I can't wait to tell the girls at school what we did Saturday night!" Debbie chortled.

"They'll never believe it," Tara added, putting her arm around Enos's broad shoulders. "Hope you don't mind, but I have to hold on to something."

"Suits me fine!" Enos smiled and winked at Jonas, whose return glance was a bit more tenuous.

36

Chapter 4

Jonas couldn't quite believe he had a cute English girl—his boss's daughter—sitting on his lap. Oh please, don't make a fool of yourself, he told himself almost prayerfully. Don't do anything stupid.

"Let's give these girls a run for their money," Enos nudged Jonas, and then muttered so the girls *almost* couldn't hear, "and give them a reason to hang on to something!"

Jonas hesitated. They were coming to a corner where they needed to turn. They should be slowing down, not picking up the pace.

"C'mon, Jonas, let's do this corner," Enos urged.

Jonas slapped the reins and Lightning picked up the pace as he approached the corner. He loved to run, so it didn't take much encouragement for Lightning to increase his speed. They took the corner on two wheels, girls screaming, Enos laughing, and Jonas praying the buggy would somehow stay upright.

"You've got more guts than I thought," Enos complimented as the horse and its buggy settled into a fast trot.

"More than I thought, too," Jonas grinned.

"Hey, show me where you live," Debbie said. Sometime during the corner turn, her arm had ended up around Jonas's shoulders.

"Oh, maybe some other time." Jonas procrastinated, thinking to himself no, not ever. Uh-uh. No way would he risk his parents seeing him with an English girl on his lap. He remembered his dad's words as they'd driven back from Wellsford on his birthday. "Don't date English girls, because what happens if you fall in love? If you should marry outside the Amish, it would break our hearts."

The breeze blowing into the buggy's open window and side door on the teens' bare arms almost felt cool. The sun had slipped beyond the horizon, leaving the clouds behind in a symphony of color.

"So, what d'ya think? Are you having a good time?" Enos switched to Pennsylvania Dutch as he addressed Jonas. Like all Amish, they'd grown up with the dialect as their native tongue, and learned English as a second language.

"Sure! How about you?"

"Great! We need another corner for you to take fast," Enos laughed. "I like it when girls get scared and need a strong body to hold onto."

"Hey, what are you guys talking about?" Debbie nudged Jonas. "That's not fair!"

"Guess!"

"I think you're talking about us. I heard a word that I think is 'girls.' Right?"

"Now what would we be saying about you?" Enos joined in.

"That's what I want to know!" Debbie shifted her weight on Jonas's leg and glanced behind them. "Look, there's a whole bunch of buggies behind us!"

"Some of the other guys," Enos noted, looking back. "They're heading for the party too. Jonas, you think we can outrun them?"

"I don't know. Their horses are fresh, and we have a heavier load. Not that you girls are big!" he added quickly.

"Let's go!" Enos encouraged.

Jonas slapped the reins sharply across the horse's back, and the gelding quickened his pace. The guys behind them were close enough to see the challenge, and urged their horses faster in response.

"I think they're gaining on us!" Debbie yelled a few minutes later. "Faster, Jonas, faster!"

But Lightning had been to Wellsford and back already that evening, and his reserves were running out. Soon three of the fastest horses were on their heels.

"Hey, where'd you get the girls?" one of the Amish guys yelled, pulling up alongside the foursome. They could hardly hear him above the racket of the two horses and eight wooden wheels racing side-by-side on the sand road.

"Connections! Jonas has connections!" Enos yelled back.

Enos's words died, drowned out in the girls' piercing screams as their buggy locked wheels with the one racing beside it. The buggy slid crazily to the left, then lurched right. Just as suddenly as they'd tangled, the wheels separated. But Jonas's young and inexperienced horse had panicked and was at a dead run. He tried desperately to pull him back, to slow down the gelding, but the reins flopped uselessly across Lightning's back.

I can't believe this, Jonas screamed inwardly. My new buggy, two English girls, and I've got a runaway!

Chapter 5
River Party

"Jonas! *Do something!*" Debbie screamed as she clung to him and the back of the seat with a white-knuckled grip, her face drained pale. "Can't you stop the horse?"

Jonas didn't answer. There was nothing he could do, and the last thing he needed was for these girls to get hurt because his horse ran away. What would Debbie's dad—his boss—say? What would his parents say? His thoughts raced ahead of the speeding horse. They were getting close to an intersection—and just around that corner was his home. He knew what would happen, and shuddered, feeling weak with fear and dread.

"We're gonna take this corner fast! You'd better bail out now!" Jonas yelled.

"We're gonna jump?" Debbie screamed.

"You've got to!" Jonas called back over the noise of the runaway. "Enos, you jump too!"

Heart racing, Jonas tried again to pull back on the lines, but Lightning controlled the rest of this ride. Then he saw the headlights of a car coming toward them in the dusk. A bad situation had just turned terrible.

"JUMP! NOW!" he ordered, an edge of hysteria cracking his voice like a whiplash.

A tumble. Terrified screams. Suddenly Jonas sat alone in the flying buggy. A quick glance over his shoulder told him the others were rolling in the ditch. At least they wouldn't be in his buggy if it met the car head on. The kids behind them, including the one they'd tangled wheels with, had stopped to help Enos and the girls.

Jonas's lathered horse and his buggy reached the corner seconds before the car did. Blinded by the head-lights, Lightning veered away from them and stumbled into the ditch. The buggy bounced crazily after him, and the next thing Jonas knew, he was laying against the jagged barbed wire fence of his dad's pasture.

"You okay?" the voice belonged to Sue Ann as she shook his shoulder.

So it was Sue Ann and Sam in the car!

"Yeah, I think so," he answered. "But Enos and two girls jumped out. Could you go check on them?"

"Sure!" Sam answered, running back to the car with Sue Ann right behind him.

Jonas stood up, noticing several deep and profusely bleeding cuts on his arm where he'd hit the sharp fence barbs. His shoulder ached, but other than that he seemed alright.

Until I get home, he thought. The worst is still coming.

He started walking the short distance to his farm, following the tracks of the crazed horse. Before he got very far, Sam's Camero pulled up beside him and stopped. The other buggies followed the car, horses snorting and dancing impatiently with the delay.

"I think you've made quite an impression on the girls," Enos laughed from the Camero. "Debbie wants to know if you carry liability insurance to pay for her hospital bills."

Jonas was thrilled to hear Enos's lighthearted words. Surely he was joking about the hospital too.

"You girls okay?" Jonas peered into the back seat.

"Pretty much so. Dirty from landing in the ditch, and we'll probably be real sore tomorrow," Debbie answered. "You've got some nasty cuts on your arm though."

"It's no big deal," Jonas covered his left arm with his right hand to conceal the bright red flow.

"Is that where you live?" Debbie pointed to the nearby farm. "Can we go there and clean up and call our parents to come get us?"

"You can wash up there," Jonas tried to hide the reluctance in his voice. "But we don't have a phone, you know."

"I can take them to Star Bowl to get their car," Sam volunteered. "Jump in, and we'll go to your place first."

"This will be interesting," Enos said in Dutch as Jonas crawled in beside him in the crowded back seat. "Your horse shows up at home with an empty buggy, and we drive in with Sam in his car, bringing two English girls with us. Are your parents home tonight?"

"Yeah, they're home. Not just them. There's a bunch of relatives there too."

Enos gave a soft, sympathetic groan.

Other than "What happened?" and "Are you all okay?" nobody said much to the teenagers as they walked into the house and took turns cleaning up in the bathroom. Nobody said much, but Jonas could feel the looks passing around the room, and knew the talk would fly as soon as they left.

"You want to go with us to take the girls to Star Bowl and then go to the party?" Sam asked Jonas and Enos when they got back to the car.

"I need to check on Lightning. If he's not hurt, we'd better drive to the party," Jonas answered. "But thanks for taking the girls back. I don't think they're ready for a buggy ride back into town."

Jonas and Enos found Lightning standing near the barn, next to the corral that held the other family horses. Although sweaty and tired, he didn't seem to have any injuries. The buggy was still hitched to him, a bit worse for the wear, but nothing was broken.

"This buggy's already getting a reputation," Enos patted the slow-moving-vehicle sign on its back. "I had no idea when we put these red lightning bolts on it that the buggy would live up to it. I thought it'd be cool to match the horse's name."

"Well, they've both had a pretty stormy time," Jonas said, leading Lightning away from the barn. "He looks alright, doesn't he?" He studied Lightning's legs as they walked across the yard. "He's fine," Enos agreed. "Let's go party! If I'm lucky, I'll buy Sol's car tonight. No more of this horse and buggy stuff for me!"

Jonas had heard that the parties along the river could get pretty wild, and this one was living up to that reputation. By midnight, nearly a hundred Amish young people were hanging out along the beach, gathered around campfires, roasting hot dogs, listening to music from car and buggy stereos, flirting, smoking and drinking. A couple of guys with cars, including Sol and his beat-up little Honda, staged drag races along the wide sandy beach. The drunker they got, the more daring the races became.

One of the races, dubbed the "Cross Country," had the cars weaving in and out of trees, driving through ditches, and crossing a shallow part of the river. Leading the pack, Sol's Honda was within a hundred yards of winning when it blew a tire. He tried to limp it in, but a hot Mustang passed him in a cloud of sand and smoke.

"Piece of junk!" Sol screamed at the car, kicking it in drunken frustration. "Worthless pile of horse crap!"

Enos, who'd been watching and cheering for Sol as he neared the finish line, swaggered through the sand to where Sol stood fuming. Although drunk, Enos could still smell an opportunity.

"Wanna sell that piece of junk? Give you a hundred dollar bill, right now."

Sol belched loudly and looked at Enos quizzically. "It's worth more than that."

"Don't know. Flat tire and all. Hundred cash right now." Enos had come prepared, hoping to deal for the car that evening. He reached into his pocket and pulled out a $100 bill. Searching

his other jeans pocket, he found a fifty. "Here, some beer money to top it off."

Sol stared at Enos, then the car. He reached out, took the $150, kicked the car one more time, and turned to stumble back to the group around the nearest campfire.

"Hot dog!" Enos let out a yell of victory.

Jonas had been sitting on a log by the fire, talking to Sue Ann during the Cross Country race. Her boyfriend, Sam, had been riding with one of the guys in the race—he knew better than to run his Camero in it because it'd tear the car up. Sue Ann admitted to Jonas that she hated the races.

"It's so stupid," she confided. "But Sam loves it—at least the ones when he can show off how fast his car is."

"It's a really nice car," Jonas agreed. "Bet it beats riding in a buggy all to heck."

"Yeah, I like it." She paused, and then added, "Sam says he'll never go back to a horse and buggy."

Jonas looked at Sue Ann. "You mean, he's going to leave the Amish?"

"Maybe. Sometime."

Jonas reached for a twig and drew meaningless sketches in the sand. Finally he said, without looking up, "and you?"

Sue Ann didn't answer for a long time. "I don't know," she said at last, and then changed the subject. "Those girls—they seemed real nice. How'd it happen you and Enos were taking them out?"

"We didn't really ask them out. Couple of weeks ago, I met Debbie at Star Bowl. She kept saying she wanted a buggy ride, so I kinda promised her one, sometime. That was before I started working at her dad's dairy. I didn't even know it was her dad when I went there the first day. Boy, was I surprised to see her out feeding the calves!"

"So you see her every day?"

"Sometimes I help her with the calves."

"So how'd it happen she and Tara were riding with you and Enos?"

"She kinda invited herself, and I didn't know how to say no." Sue Ann's dark eyes danced with laughter. "My, my, Jonas. You've just started running with the young folks, and already you're having to fight off English girls. What kind of special charm do you have anyway?"

Jonas blushed. The best-looking girl he'd ever seen was teasing him about other girls. She may be going steady with Sam, but it didn't make her any less attractive to him. And it didn't mean they couldn't be friends.

"Gonna take my new car out for a spin!" Enos's sour beer breath nearly sickened Jonas. "Wanna go along?"

"No thanks. And you shouldn't go either. You're drunk, Enos."

"Don't matter. It's my car. Bought it for 150 big ones. And I can drive it if I want to."

"Don't do it, Enos. You're wasted!"

"Not wasted. I even changed the tire. Put that rinky dink tricycle tire on. Gonna see how fast it'll go!"

Jonas stood up from the log he'd been sitting on near Sue Ann. Suddenly, without a word, he sprinted towards the Honda, flung open the door, and grabbed the keys from the ignition.

"Gimme those keys!" Enos yelled, stumbling towards Jonas and the car.

"No, you're not driving 'til you sober up."

"Gimme!"

"No."

"You stupid jerk, Jonas. I CAN DRIVE A CAR DRUNK BETTER THAN YOU CAN DRIVE A HORSE WHEN YOU'RE SOBER!"

Enos's loud voice attracted the attention of a few of the people around him, but most of them didn't care or were crashed near the campfires. Sam had joined Sue Ann on her blanket, and he got up to talk to Enos.

"Get some sleep, buddy." Sam guided Enos away from where Jonas stood. "You can drive your car in the morning."

Jonas walked to his buggy to get a blanket to sleep on. He didn't mind Enos's insult so much, except that it reminded him again of the runaway. Either his dad, or Harlan, or both, were bound to make things miserable for him.

Unlike many of the young people at the party, he hadn't deliberately done anything that could get him in trouble. Yet he knew he'd be facing the music, come Monday.

Chapter 6
Aftermath

"So, how was the party?"

Startled, Jonas looked up from the milker he was taking off a cow, and saw Debbie standing behind him.

"Don't sneak up on me like that. I'm liable to find a way to get back at you," he warned and grinned up at her.

"Like throw me off a buggy?" Debbie teased in return.

"Hey, I'm really sorry about that. Are you okay?"

"A little sore, but that's all. I think you got the worst end of the deal," she said, nodding at the cuts on his arm. "You sure have a great tan already," she added, thinking to herself, on such strong, muscular arms!

"Never thought about getting tan," Jonas glanced down at his arms. "Guess it just happens."

"Tell me about the party!" Debbie enthused.

"Oh, it was just a bunch of Amish kids hanging out, eating, drinking, racing cars, playing cards, that kind of thing."

"Racing cars? Drinking? That sounds kinda wild for Amish people, doesn't it?"

"Not for the young folks. It's pretty normal, I guess."

"But your church is so strict about everything. How can they let the teens do that kind of stuff?"

"I don't know. I mean, it's not like they *like* what the young folks do. But it's tradition. Our parents did it when they were young, and probably their parents before them. Well, maybe not the cars. But from the stories I've heard, you can raise a lot of Cain with a horse and buggy too."

Chapter 6

Jonas had been moving along the row of cows as they talked, taking milkers off as he went. When he reached the end of the barn, he crossed to the other side and began going down that side. Debbie followed along, intrigued with what he was saying.

"Tell me some of the stories you've heard!"

"Ah, not now."

"C'mon, Jonas, just one."

She has a way of getting what she wants out of me, Jonas thought. His blue eyes met her teasing green ones, and he gave in.

"Okay, just one. My dad tells a story about him and a bunch of other guys with horses and buggies. They went into town one night, and during the middle of the night, they decided to take their horses to the golf course."

"The golf course?"

"Uh-huh. They took them across the greens, and tried to make them take a crap on the greens."

"You're kidding! Did they?"

"I don't think so. But a cop caught them at it. He wanted to haul them all in for destroying public property, but he didn't know what to do with all of the horses. So he escorted the guys out of town, red lights, sirens, and everything, and told them if he caught them in town after curfew again, they'd be in big trouble."

"I can see it now. A whole line of horses and buggies leaving town, under police escort, at 3:00 in the morning. It must have been hilarious!"

"My dad and his friends laughed about it for a long time. 'Course now if I'd ever do something like that, he wouldn't be laughing," Jonas grew sober, thinking about what awaited him that evening. He'd left before breakfast, and still hadn't talked to his parents since the weekend accident with Enos and the girls.

"Parents are all the same when it comes to that," Debbie

agreed. "I think they're paranoid about what we're doing because they did it themselves as kids. My parents wouldn't let me date until I was 16. I was so mad, because I had a boyfriend in school that I really wanted to go out with. But no! I couldn't date yet. Now I'm 16, and I'm not with that guy anymore. Finally I'm old enough, and I'm not dating." Debbie paused. "Have you dated a lot?"

"Hardly," Jonas chuckled. "But I will. I've just started running with the young folks, you know. I'll have a date every weekend from now on."

"You mean you have an Amish girlfriend already?"

"Are you kidding? No, I don't have an Amish girlfriend."

"Then what do you mean, you'll 'have a date every weekend'?"

"Just that. We all do. Different guys take different girls out every weekend. We end up dating 'most everybody at least once, I guess."

"That's weird. You mean you don't have any kind of commitment to a certain girl?"

"Not until you decide to go steady. And going steady means you're probably going to get married."

"Wow, that *is* strange. That's not at all what going steady usually means."

"It does for us," Jonas said a bit defensively, taking the milker off of the last cow. He hung the milker up, and slapped the cow on the rump. She knew the signal, and ambled toward the door, swatting flies with her tail as she went. The other cows in the milking parlor followed her lead, and Jonas began washing the milkers.

Debbie watched for a few minutes, then turned to leave. "Gotta go feed the calves," she said.

Jonas helped Harlan with fieldwork that day after the morning milking, and he almost offered to stay around after the evening chores too. Driving Harlan's big air-conditioned John

Deere tractor and listening to a Kansas City Royals ball game sounded like a great way to spend the muggy May evening. Especially when the alternative was his home, where the conversation around the supper table would probably be about as hot as the house itself. But he decided to get it over with, and Debbie wished him good luck as he left the farmyard on Lightning for the hour-long ride home.

Lightning trotted into the farmyard and stopped in front of the barn, impatient to get out into the pasture for a drink and to roll his sweat-drenched body in the dirt. Jonas slid off Lightning's bare back, his jeans sticking to his seat and legs. He'd been riding bareback almost as long as he'd been walking, but he still didn't like the feeling of sweat-wet pants.

The family tomcat sauntered out of the barn toward Jonas, and rubbed his head against Jonas's ankle. Turning around Jonas's legs, he bumped them again.

"Yes, Red, I see you," Jonas said. "You've been gone again. The girls keeping you busy?"

Hearing his name, Red responded with a meow. He was one of their "talking cats"—he seemed to enjoy having "conversations" with family members.

"You're lucky, you know," Jonas said.

"Meow."

Jonas looked around before continuing. "How? Your love life. It's so uncomplicated."

"Meow."

"I don't even *have* a love life, and it's a mess already."

Red rubbed against Jonas again, threw back a final meow, and strolled back into the barn, his fluffy reddish-gold tail flicking back and forth.

Jonas led Lightning through the pasture gate and turned him loose. Then he began walking slowly toward the house.

Jonas's mother, Esther, was frying chicken when he came into the kitchen. No electricity meant no air-conditioning, not even fans to move the air around. Beads of sweat collected on Esther's forehead and upper lip, and her dark blue dress showed the sweat and dirt of a hard day's work. She looked up and smiled slightly at her oldest son.

"Supper will be ready soon," she said. "Round up the rest of the kids."

Jonas sneaked a peek at his family during the long silent supper prayer. Across the table from him were his three younger brothers. David and Orie had their heads bowed, but Robert's clear blue eyes met Jonas's and winked at him. Jonas looked toward his father at one end of the table, his bent head sending his long beard halfway down his chest. To his left, out of the corner of his eye, he could see Rebecca and Roseanne, their white prayer cap strings dangling beside their lowered faces. Around the table corner from him, his mother prayed, elbows on the table and her head resting on folded hands. She's probably praying about me, he thought uneasily. And then he wondered why he'd even thought that at all.

Prayer was an important aspect of Amish religious life, but rarely had he heard it expressed in the form of personal prayers for another person. Silent prayer was offered to God before and after every meal. The whole family gathered every night before going to bed, knelt in the living room, and recited a German prayer together. The only prayers Jonas had ever heard, whether at home or in church, were recited ones. What happened in the personal prayer life of his parents, he didn't know. They never talked about it.

Fred raised his head and shifted slightly in his chair, and the family followed the cue. Plates of fried chicken, mashed potatoes, tapioca pudding, green beans, bread and butter awaited them.

"Who was that girl with you Saturday night?" Orie asked. "She didn't look like anybody *I* know."

"She's Harlan's daughter," Jonas studied the platter of chicken being passed to him. "She begged for a buggy ride, so I gave her one." Might as well get the facts out, he figured.

"You sure did!" Rebecca giggled. "Bet she doesn't ask again!"

"Be fine with me," Jonas muttered.

"Were they with you young folks the rest of the evening?" Fred asked, looking directly at Jonas.

"No, Sam took them back to town. Their car was at Star Bowl."

"And they didn't come back out to wherever you all were partying?"

"No! I said that already."

"Okay, okay. Don't get so huffy. Just curious, that's all," Fred said, and then added, almost under his breath, "curious, like those English girls."

Jonas didn't know what had gotten into his father, but he didn't like it. After supper, he followed Fred out of the house. He was crazy to bring it up again, but his father's comment bugged him. Bad.

"What did you mean, 'curious, like those English girls'?" he asked as they walked towards the wheat binder. Harvest wasn't far away, and they had repairs to do before the equipment was ready. Jonas noted the setting sun—they had about an hour before dark.

"I warned you against dating English girls. Remember?" Fred answered, opening up his tool box beside the binder.

"This wasn't a date! She asked for a ride, and I gave it to her!"

"Yeah, and if she wants another one? What else will she be asking you? Next she'll want to take you out in her car. I'm not stupid, Jonas. I know you probably see her around the farm every day. I wish I'd known this when I took you there for that job."

"Look, Dad, you're putting a lot into this that isn't there. Believe me!" Jonas was suddenly getting scared he'd have to quit the job.

"Maybe it isn't there yet, but things happen, Jonas. If you and that girl should get together, and someday marry, you wouldn't be happy. I'm not saying they aren't good people. They are. But you were born Amish, and you would be disobeying God if you left. As your father, it is my responsibility to bring you up right. I would never forgive myself if I failed."

"But Dad—"

"And if someday, I would have a granddaughter sitting on my lap that didn't understand me when I talked Dutch to her, that would hurt me a lot. She'd grow up in a world of TV, drugs in school, who knows what else. She'd probably be wearing those short shorts when she comes to see us—if she'd come."

Jonas couldn't believe his ears. Surely his dad had slipped into his tongue-in-cheek humor somewhere along the way. Fred's next statement made it clear he hadn't.

"And someday, how awful it would be if one of my own children was driving a car in my funeral procession."

Fred looked up, and Jonas saw pain in his father's eyes—an emotional pain he'd never seen before. For Jonas, the seeming improbability of his dad's scenario paled in comparison to the hurt he was expressing. He didn't know what to say, so he said nothing as they worked side by side until darkness forced them to quit for the night.

Chapter 7
Boundaries

Wheat harvest in June meant a lot of extra work at the Schmidt dairy, and Harlan asked Jonas if he'd be willing to help with the farm work in addition to his milking duties. Jonas agreed willingly, and often spent 16-hour days at the Schmidt farm. After riding his horse home from work, he'd exchange a few words with his family and fall into bed. By 5:00 a.m. he'd be leaving again.

"Why don't you get your license?" Debbie asked Jonas over lunch one day. "Other Amish guys have theirs, just to drive to and from work."

Jonas, who'd been eating meals with the Schmidt family for several weeks, fidgeted in his chair. It was one thing for them to open their home to him and invite him to their table. It was another thing for him to openly share about his life and his relationship with his parents. Especially on topics where they disagreed. It wouldn't be respectful.

On the other hand, he reflected, this time-consuming riding back and forth every day is sure getting old.

"My dad won't let me," Jonas answered without looking up.

"Funny thing is, your dad drove when he was a teenager," Harlan said with a chuckle. "And he did more than drive to and from work. If the car he drove could talk, it'd have some stories to tell!"

"Really, Dad! What did Jonas's dad do?" Debbie was all ears.

"Well, first of all, a group of Amish guys—and Fred was one

of them—pooled their money and bought this big old boat of a car. Only one of them had a license at the time. It wasn't Fred—he got his later. But when they left the car lot, Fred was the one driving. I think there were about ten other guys in the car, if I remember right. Believe me, that was one heck of a ride!"

"How do you know?" Jonas couldn't help asking.

Harlan reached across the table and playfully punched Jonas on the shoulder. "Because I was in that car!"

So, Fred and Harlan knew each other when they were kids, Jonas and Debbie realized simultaneously.

"I bet you can tell a lot more stories about his dad!" Debbie enthused.

"I can, but I won't. At least not now," Harlan winked. "But about your driving. Did he absolutely forbid you to get your license?"

"Yep," Jonas answered. "And then he said that if you wanted me to work so bad, you could pick me up."

And that's how it happened that Debbie began to drive Jonas to and from work. Jonas could tell his parents weren't thrilled with the arrangement, but they didn't say anything. *Dad knows he said they could pick me up—he just didn't know it'd be Debbie doing it,* Jonas thought to himself. *And they won't make me quit, because I'm bringing in good money for the family.*

The summer flew by in a flurry of work and weekends. The more time Jonas spent with the Schmidts, the more at ease he felt with the family. He and Debbie shared a comfortable friendship, although at times Jonas sensed she wanted it to be more. Harlan obviously liked Jonas, and was keeping the promise he made the day he hired him.

"How about a heifer calf this time?" Harlan asked Jonas as they inspected the young black and white calves one morning in September. Each calf was tied to its own square white hut, and Jonas enjoyed walking through the three neat rows of huts and calves. The hungry calves could be totally obnoxious, bawling loudly, then tipping the buckets in their frenzy when Debbie or Jonas brought the milk. But Jonas still enjoyed the baby Holsteins, and he smiled broadly at Harlan's question.

"Well, sure, whatever you say," he answered. "But don't you keep the heifers as replacement cows for your herd?"

"Yeah, I do," Harlan agreed as he continued strolling through the rows of huts and calves. "But I've been watching you with the cows. You're good. Who knows, someday you might want your own dairy. Thought I'd give you a start. She's a few years from being a great milk cow," Harlan said, stopping at a shiny little black calf with a white face and big dark eyes. "But she's yours, and you can keep her and feed her here."

"Thanks, Harlan. She's beautiful," Jonas let the calf nuzzle and suck on his fingers. "Now I'll really have to work hard for you!"

"Hey, you have been! You've been putting in crazy long hours all summer! Are you still giving all the money to your dad? Can't you keep some of it when you're working so much?"

"Not really. I just turn the check you give me over to him. I get some spending money from him though. And he bought me that buggy, you know, and gave me Lightning."

"Well, it doesn't seem quite fair anyhow," Harlan said, stopping at the last calf and looking it over closely. His experienced eyes and nose told him the little bull calf had a problem. "Got some dysentery here. Need to treat him right away. You know how fast they can die at this age."

His gaze turned towards Jonas. "Have you ever thought about leaving?"

"Leaving?"

"The Amish. You're bright, responsible. You could go on to school. College, even. Did you ever think about it?"

"No, not really."

"You should," Harlan said matter-of-factly. "But first, treat the sick one here. Who knows? Maybe you'll want to be a vet."

Jonas thought about his conversation with Harlan later that afternoon while working one of the fields, getting it ready to plant wheat. For one thing, he really appreciated Harlan's kindness and generosity. Giving him a heifer calf was no small deal—when full grown and ready to be bred, she'd be worth around $1,000. And then there was the way Harlan kept challenging Jonas about certain Amish things—like giving his money to his parents and not being able to drive. But today he'd really surprised him with that question about leaving the Amish. And then suggesting he go on to school? College? Be a vet?

Impossible. Jonas shrugged it off. Some things about being Amish, the English just couldn't understand.

Like weekends. He couldn't talk to the Schmidts about what he did on weekends because they wouldn't understand. He wasn't always sure he did! He enjoyed leaving home Saturday night and being gone with the young folks until sometime late Sunday/ early Monday morning. He'd even started drinking, although something kept him from downing enough to get wasted, like a lot of the other kids. And yes, he'd had a different girl every weekend, just like he'd told Debbie he would.

But a few things nagged at Jonas. Enos's heavy drinking bothered him. And too often while drunk, Enos got into his car and drove like crazy. Some of the other guys did too, but Enos was the worst.

The other worrisome thought was harder to pinpoint. All his life, he'd been raised to believe that his people, the Amish, were people of God. He didn't know exactly what that meant, but somehow it tied in with their strict lifestyle, and with not having "worldly" things. At the same time, as a child, he'd somehow figured that if the Amish were the people of God, then the English weren't.

Now, at 16, Jonas felt two things challenging those black and white boundaries. First, it seemed confusing that the teenagers of the "people of God" could do such wild and rowdy things. Secondly, the Schmidt family seemed to have something going with God too. They prayed together before they ate. They talked about the sermon they'd heard in church. Debbie belonged to a group of young people in her church that had a lot of fun, as well as studying the Bible together.

So, while Jonas found himself questioning the only religion he'd ever known, he was also asking questions about Christianity in general. Could a person be Presbyterian—like the Schmidts—and be closer to God than the Amish? Would a person even *want* to be close to God?

He didn't know. Most of what he remembered hearing about God in sermons scared him. God punished those who strayed. God demanded loyalty and faithfulness, and the "wages of sin is death." He wanted to be on the "good" side of God, but beyond that? Uh-uh.

One Saturday early in October, Jonas asked Harlan if he could take the afternoon off to help Enos fix his car. Harlan said "Sure," and Debbie drove him to Enos's home.

"The car's a disaster, but Enos thinks he's taking it to a party in Oklahoma," Jonas explained to Debbie on the way over.

"And what do you two Amish guys know about fixing a car?" Debbie asked in her usual teasing way. Jonas liked the way Debbie could give a person a hard time, all in a fun-loving spirit.

"Good question," he answered. "Very little. I guess we're hoping two dumb heads are better than one."

"Well, I hope you're better with cars than runaway buggies!" Debbie couldn't resist the lighthearted dig as she stopped the car at the end of Enos's lane.

"Hey, give me a break!" Jonas laughed in return. "Thanks for the ride!"

Jonas spotted the rusty brown car behind a row of trees along the north side of the farmyard. Enos's family knew he had the car, and they didn't like it. Enos didn't care what they thought, but he respected his father enough to "hide" the car to some degree. As Jonas walked toward the trees, he could see Enos crouched next to a back wheel of the car.

"So what's wrong?" Jonas knelt down beside Enos.

"Brakes."

"Can't say I know much about them."

"Me neither."

"So how're we gonna fix them?"

"Got some baling wire here. Think that'll do?"

Jonas knew Enos was joking. On the other hand, Enos probably would have repaired the brakes with cheap wire if he could. Sighing, Jonas picked up the tire wrench.

"So what's the plan with this trip to Oklahoma?" Jonas asked as he began to loosen a bolt.

"We go, we get dates, we party, we come back," Enos laughed.

"Who all's going?"

"I'm driving and taking a load of guys. You and whoever else wants to go—I figure we can get seven in this baby," he tapped the bottom of the old Honda.

"Seven? In here? For six hours?"

"Guess you can't bring much luggage! We'll just pile in and go!"

Jonas knew all about "piling in." Large Amish families traveled together in their two-seated buggies all the time. While the rest of the world hurried to buy mini vans for families of two or three children, the Amish managed to pack parents and as many children as God sent them into their no-frills, front-and-back-seat buggies.

"I suppose you're going to tell me we're taking half a dozen girls in our car too," Jonas deadpanned.

"Sounds good to me! Actually, I think they're going in a van. I heard that Sue Ann works with someone at the restaurant that agreed to drive a bunch of the girls down."

"Aren't Sue Ann and Sam driving?"

"Sam's not going because he has to work that weekend. But Sue Ann is. Here's your chance, Jonas."

"What do you mean?"

"I know you're sweet on her. C'mon, admit it."

"I'm not. Besides, she's going steady with Sam."

Jonas's conscience twinged even as he said the words. He'd never met a girl who stirred his insides when she talked to him the way Sue Ann did. But she was two years older, and she'd been going steady with Sam since spring. They had to be serious—they'd probably get married next spring. Amish weddings often happened in spring and fall. This fall was too soon for Sue Ann and Sam—they hadn't even joined the church yet. And what had she said at the river party—the one when Enos bought his car and Jonas talked for a long time with Sue Ann? Something about Sam not joining the Amish? Would Sue Ann leave too in order to marry him?

"Well, he's not going to be in Oklahoma, and you are," Enos interrupted Jonas's thoughts.

"Yeah, right," was all Jonas said.

Chapter 8

Halloween

Fred and Esther weren't thrilled about Jonas going to Oklahoma with Enos for the weekend, and they made it clear. Oklahoma wasn't the problem—in fact, they liked the idea of Jonas meeting girls from another Amish community. The health and well-being of Amish people depended on dating and marriages between communities.

Riding with Enos—that's what they feared. Jonas's parents didn't trust Enos, and they had less faith in his car. Jonas wouldn't admit it to them, but he agreed with his parents. Although he somewhat dreaded the crowded trip with a crazy driver in an unreliable car, he felt someone responsible should be along. Just exactly what that might mean, he didn't know. At any rate, he told his parents he was going. End of discussion.

So, early in the morning on the last Saturday in October—Halloween, in fact—Enos, Jonas and five other guys sandwiched themselves into the little brown car and headed south. The mini van of girls followed them for the six-hour drive to the Amish settlement near Millersburg in central Oklahoma.

Upon their arrival, Enos's carload and the van went to separate farms—homes of teenagers in the community—where lunch awaited them. After eating and getting reacquainted with some of the local young folks, they drove into Millersburg and checked into three motel rooms. "One for the guys, one for the girls, and one for all the couples," Enos's eyes teased the middle-aged woman at the front desk who was registering him. "But we'll be quiet! I promise!"

The woman gazed at Enos over her reading glasses, and then stared at the snickering teens around him. "We'll hold you responsible for your group, young man. Any excessive noise— we call the cops. Damages to the room—you pay. Understood?"

The woman's abrupt manner caught Enos by surprise, but not for long.

"Yes, ma'am. We will be good, *ma'am*," he saluted her smartly and then turned on his heels. "Forward march, troops!"

The group marched out behind him, barely containing their explosive laughter until they got outside the door. As he left the lobby, Jonas heard the desk clerk mutter something about "crazy Amish kids—worse than prom night."

Rooms secured, the teenagers invaded a video store and rented VCRs and enough movies to last them for days.

"Might as well watch some movies now before it gets dark, 'cause then we'll have other things to do," Enos said as they drove back to the motel. The rest of the guys agreed knowingly, so they invited the girls to their room and the 14 teens laughed their way through two Eddie Murphy videos.

By supper time, two dozen local teens showed up at the motel, and the group ordered pizza delivered to their rooms. Amidst thick slices of pepperoni pizza, they discussed plans for the rest of the evening and night.

The next morning, the Ben Schrock family of the Millersburg Amish community arose long before daybreak. They were having church in their home that Sunday, and many last-minute chores and details awaited them. So did a few surprises.

During the night, their entire homestead had been wrapped in toilet paper. The house, barn, outbuildings, trees, livestock fences—nothing escaped the Halloween pranksters.

Not even the livestock. When Ben hurried out to his barn to

do the morning milking, he immediately noticed a strange still-ness. Shining his Coleman lantern into the corral outside the barn, Ben's heart sank. Rather than the friendly black and white faces of his Holsteins waiting to be milked, only blackness greeted him. Muttering under his breath, he broke into a run through the corral and the open gate to the pasture—the gate he knew he'd closed the night before.

66

Chapter
8

Ben could hear the cows mooing in the darkness, and won-dered why, if they'd been let out into the pasture, they hadn't returned on their own as milking time neared. The light from his lantern soon cleared up the mystery.

The cows stood huddled in a corner of the pasture. A crude but strong makeshift fence of wire panels completed the enclo-sure. And yes, toilet paper adorned the four sides of the pen.

At noon that same day, a housekeeper at the Millersburg Motor Inn knocked on the door of one of the rooms rented by the Amish kids the day before. Since it was an hour past check-out time and no one responded, she opened the door with her master key. She let out an audible groan at the scene in front of her.

Sleeping teens occupied all of the bed and floor space. Strewn between them were aluminum cans, pizza boxes and crusts, video tapes, toilet paper, clothes, potato chips, playing cards, etc. One of the boys stirred and opened his eyes. He did a double take when he saw the woman in the doorway.

"What time is it?" Jonas asked, rubbing his eyes.

"12:00. Check-out time was an hour ago," she replied. "You'll be lucky if they don't charge you for an extra day," she said, turn-ing and slamming the door behind her.

"Now what?" Enos grumbled at Jonas as they packed them-selves and the other guys in the car. "I thought we could stay there all day. We didn't even watch all the movies."

"We take the movies and the machine back, I guess. One of the guys said something last night about going out to somebody's pasture today. We could pick up some hot dogs and roast them."

"Yeah, the local kids said we should meet them there," a voice from the back seat added. "I think I know where it is."

Enos's carload of guys and the girls in the van stopped at the grocery store, picked up food and drinks for lunch, and then left Millersburg for the party in the pasture.

"Brakes seem to be holding up," Jonas commented as they roared out of town. "But I still say you should have taken the car into a shop rather than fixing them yourself."

"Hey, we did it, didn't we?" Enos responded. "Probably saved ourselves a hundred bucks in the process. Do I need to prove to you how good these brakes are?"

Before Jonas could answer, the car accelerated up to 70 mph.

"Enos!"

Eighty...

"Enos! Slow down!"

Ninety...

"Amazing this little thing can do this, and full of guys too!" Enos yelled above the wind rushing through their open windows. "Now, watch these brakes!"

"ENOS, DON'T!" Jonas screamed.

"Okay, okay," Enos pulled his foot from the accelerator. "You don't have to get so shook up!"

Amidst loud recollections of escapades with cows and toilet paper during the night, the one guy who supposedly knew where to go instructed Enos on where to turn. Sometimes he let Enos know before the corner arrived, sometimes he didn't, making it all the more fun for them, and challenging for the van trying to follow behind.

"I think we're almost there," the voice came from the back seat. "Maybe just over that next hill."

"Don't have hills back home," Enos said, pushing the accelerator. "Gotta have fun with them when we can!"

As Enos and the guys crested the hill, they noticed a horse and buggy ahead of them, halfway down the hill. Three young people—a guy and two girls—sat in the open-seated buggy. Enos hit the brakes gradually, fully confident his car would slow down enough not to rear-end them.

But nothing happened.

Jonas glanced at Enos, whose white-knuckled hands gripped the steering wheel. His usually jovial face reflected shear fear and panic now. He pushed the brakes again, all the way to the floor.

Still nothing.

In the seconds before impact, Jonas heard his parents' warnings about riding with Enos, he remembered telling Enos to take the car in to fix the brakes, he could hear the bishop intoning "the wages of sin is death, the wages of sin is death," and he heard himself screaming as the small brown car flew into and wedged under the taller buggy. Wood splintered, metal creaked, and there were awful fleshy thumps as the buggy's occupants catapulted into the air and bounced over the car hood as it rolled under them. The teenagers landed on the road with bone-jarring impact as the car, smelling of gas and hot oil, continued on, slamming into the confused and terrified horse. Together, the car and horse skidded to a sickening stop at the bottom of the hill.

An eerie stillness filled the car for a moment, and then the guys began untangling themselves and crawling out the doors. Bruised and bleeding from superficial wounds, they quickly checked for more serious injuries and didn't find any. Then they looked back up the hill.

The girls' van, following behind them, had narrowly missed the three teens lying on the road like discarded ragdolls. The girls were helping move the injured young people off the road and into the grassy ditch.

Jonas glanced at the horse wedged under the front of the car. Blood was seeping from its mouth and bubbling from its nostrils.

His wildly rolling eyes reflected terror and pain. Without warning, his body gave a large convulsion, and the heavy breathing stopped as the spasm ended. The eyes stared, no longer hurting, no longer seeing. Dead... Jonas turned away, caught in a nightmare from which there was no awakening.

"Sue Ann!" he yelled, running up the hill. "Are they okay?"

"They're all conscious, but banged up pretty bad," Sue Ann answered as Jonas approached. "How do you all feel?" she addressed the trio, looking from one to another, urging answers and assurances.

"I'm okay," the guy stood up somewhat shakily. "But what about..." his voice trailed off as he stared down the hill.

He took off running towards the still form of his horse. While the rest of the group watched, he knelt down beside the big black gelding. Moments later, he stood up with a loud curse, his eyes glaring and glistening with unshed tears of loss and fury.

"You killed my horse!" he screamed at Enos. Striding to the car, he kicked it violently, then turned and began running away from them down the road, as if trying to outdistance grief and reality.

"Will raised that horse from a colt," one of the girls who'd been with him said in a miserable whisper. "Broke him to drive himself. That horse meant everything to Will."

They watched silently as Will continued his angry, grief-stricken run away from them and the horse he loved.

The van driver took Sue Ann and Jonas to a nearby farm to call an ambulance, and with the help of the farmer and his tractor, the guys saw to it that the horse's body and Enos's car were off the road and out of the way. Then the mini van, now packed with all 14 Kansas teens, continued down the road to the pasture.

Will's distressed arrival there had informed the local youth of the accident, changing the mood dramatically. While most of them roasted hot dogs and ate listlessly, the van driver offered to take a few kids to the hospital and to bring the local girls home after being released. They arrived back at the pasture late in the afternoon. One of the girls had a broken collarbone, the other was being kept in the hospital for observation. Will was bruised and cut, but his physical injuries paled in comparison to the emotional pain he was going through.

With Enos's car wrecked, the guys joined the girls in their van for the trip home. Fourteen people in a seven-passenger van could have been fun under better circumstances, but this time the drive seemed endless. For Jonas, the only good thing about it was that the crowded conditions forced Sue Ann to sit on his lap.

"Remember what I told you?" Enos winked at Jonas, his eyes shifting to Sue Ann. "Remember?"

Jonas couldn't believe Enos was joking about Sue Ann sitting on his lap. Not with his car wreck being the cause of the circumstances. Not with the cloud of pain they'd left behind in the Oklahoma community.

"I remember telling you to take that car in to have the brakes fixed," Jonas answered curtly.

"Oh, give me a break, man," Enos laughed. "Get it? Break! Brake!"

"Shut up, Enos," Sue Ann stepped in. "None of us feels like hearing you run off at the mouth right now. You're not funny."

Surprised, Enos scrutinized Sue Ann, then Jonas, then the rest of the stuffed van. "Okay, okay, I'm needing a nap anyway," he said, leaning his head against the window. "Wake me when we get home."

News of the accident traveled fast upon the van's arrival back in Wellsford. And as usual, the news grew along its journey from house to house, friend to friend, relative to relative. Jonas fully expected to hear the "I told you so" speech from his parents when he told them about the accident, but they didn't say much. As far as the other Halloween happenings, Jonas didn't see any need to tell them about the pranks.

"What all did you kids do in Oklahoma anyway?" Fred confronted Jonas several days later. "I'm hearing all kinds of things from other people—things you didn't tell us. Did you guys really let Ben Schrock's cattle out, chase them down the road to the neighbor's, and pen them up with their herd? And the day they were having church? Have you no respect for people or for church Sunday?"

"We didn't let them out and chase them to the neighbor's," Jonas answered defensively. "We put them in the pasture and built a pen around them, that's all."

"It's still disrespectful."

Like you never did anything crazy as a kid, Jonas thought to himself.

"And then you T.P.'d the whole farmyard?" Fred continued.

"Yeah."

"How in the world did you manage that without somebody hearing you? Didn't their dog bark?" Jonas wasn't sure, but he thought he detected a hint of curious admiration in his father's voice.

"Couple of the girls brought some treats for him—kept him quiet," Jonas admitted. "As far as the toilet paper—you'd be surprised how quiet we can be when we have to," he dared a half-smile at his dad.

"Yeah, I believe that," Fred nodded. "So does this mean we have to hide our toilet paper from you every time we're going to have church here?"

Jonas caught the old familiar twinkle in his dad's eyes—the one he hadn't seen for a long time.

"That's okay, we can bring our own if we have to."

Chapter 9

New Year's Eve

"**I**sn't it hard to give him a shot?" Debbie asked Jonas as he deftly stuck the syringe needle in the day-old calf's hip.

"Guess I've done it so much I don't think about it," he answered. "And if we have to do it to keep him alive, it's worth it."

The late December north wind whipped around the small calf hut that Debbie and Jonas crouched behind as they tended to the sick calf. Cold weather didn't bother healthy calves, but when they did get sick, they had more trouble fighting off pneumonia in the frigid conditions.

"I'd still have trouble doing it," Debbie continued, holding a milk bucket for the calf to drink. He nuzzled at it listlessly. "I think you can give him shots because you're more calloused about animals. Like the way you Amish drive your horses. In cold weather, you drive them for miles, they get all hot and sweaty and then you stop someplace and they stand there for hours in the cold. That's gotta be hard on them. I don't think you feel for animals like I do," she said, backing away from the calf. "He's not drinking. We'll probably have to tube-feed him."

"Probably," Jonas answered. "Why don't you go get it while I give a few more shots?"

While she was gone, Jonas thought about Debbie's comments on how the Amish treated their horses, and her accusation that he didn't like animals as much as she did. When she returned with the stomach-tube, she held it while he poured some of the milk from the bucket into the heavy plastic bag at the top of the feeder. The bag was attached to a clear plastic hose. A clamp between the bag and the hose regulated the flow of the milk.

"It's not true about all Amish being calloused toward their animals," Jonas said as he inserted the hose in the calf's mouth. He carefully pushed the tube down the calf's throat until he knew, because it wouldn't go any farther, that it had reached the stomach. "I never told you what happened on Halloween weekend when a bunch of us went to Oklahoma."

Jonas slowly released the clamp and watched as the milk flowed through the tube. "The brakes went out on Enos's car and we hit some kids with their horse and buggy. The kids were okay, but it killed the horse. A big beautiful black horse." Jonas paused. "Bad thing about it, it was a horse that Will, the driver, had raised from a colt. I've never seen anyone so upset about something happening to a horse. I couldn't get it off my mind—not just Will's crying, but I kept seeing that horse in the middle of the road. I kept seeing his eyes, and the way he died...." Jonas's voice trailed off. The milk was all in the calf's stomach, and Jonas pulled the tube out.

Debbie watched silently. Finally, she touched Jonas's shoulder and said softly, "I'm sorry. I didn't mean what I said."

Jonas shrugged his shoulders, but didn't look at Debbie. He couldn't let their eyes meet. Not right then.

They walked in silence toward the barn.

"I'm having some kids over on New Year's Eve. You wanna come?" Debbie asked Jonas as she drove him home later that evening.

"Me? At your party? Naw, I don't think so."

"Why not? It's no big deal—just some food, movies, that kind of thing. Believe me, it won't be as wild as what you're used to! Or is that why you don't want to come? Aren't we fun enough for you?" she was starting to tease.

"No, that's not it. I just don't know any of the other kids."

"You know *me*. And the others are easy to get to know. Tara's going to be there—she's been asking about you ever since that buggy ride last summer. The party'll be over by 1:00 'cause that's when my parents will come home from the one they're going to. So you can leave and still make it to your Amish all-nighter. What do you think?"

"I don't know. I'll have to think about it. I'll let you know tomorrow."

Jonas left home on New Year's Eve with his horse and buggy. He knew his parents were probably wondering why, since Enos usually picked him up with his car, and he'd bought another one after the fateful weekend in Oklahoma. As usual, Jonas offered no explanation of where he was going or when he'd be home. He just left, turning Lightning's head into the wind for the cold ride into Wellsford.

He still didn't really know why he'd told Debbie yes yesterday. Why *was* he going to her New Year's Eve party?

Curiosity, I guess, he mused, taking off a glove so he could pick a tape out of the box sitting on the seat beside him. He slipped the tape into the cassette player in the wooden dash in the buggy. Mary Chapin Carpenter's voice rocked out of the speakers in front of him.

"I feel lucky, I feel lucky today," the female country singer blasted.

By the time Lightning pulled the buggy up at the bowling alley's hitching post, his coat shone with sweat, and Jonas was chilled to the bone. Jonas grabbed the horse blanket he'd been sitting on and jumped out of the buggy. He'd show Debbie what a calloused Amish guy he wasn't, he thought, laying the blanket over the horse from his shoulders to rump. He tied it with some twine, and then ran for the warmth of the bowling alley.

Two hot chocolates and 20 minutes later, Jonas's feet and fingers felt normal again. His heart jumped when someone touched his arm.

"Hey, good-lookin', you lookin' for a good time?" Jonas turned to see Debbie's teasing smile and twinkling eyes.

"Sure, why not?" he answered. What the heck, he thought, let's see what your parties are all about. The twosome stepped out into the cold and walked to Debbie's car.

"Let's swing around the corner and check Lightning," Jonas said as Debbie backed the car up. Normally he wouldn't do that, but he had his reasons this time.

"Hey, he's got a blanket on!" Debbie exclaimed as the car lights hit the horse tied to the hitching post.

"Don't want to leave the impression that I'm cruel and cold-hearted," Jonas said, and now the teasing was in his voice.

"Hey, I said I was sorry," Debbie responded. "I don't think that at all," she reached over and touched his knee. "I know you have a kind heart."

"Okay, just wanted to make sure," Jonas said and flashed a smile that was lost in the darkness of the car.

They left town silently, both sensing that this evening was different than all of the time they'd spent together on the farm. Jonas felt like he should do or say something, but his insides were going crazy. He'd dated Amish girls, sure, and even made out with them. But that was almost a game—just something they did. This was different. This was Debbie—the girl he fed calves with every day, the one who drove him to and from work, the daughter of his boss, a "worldly girl" like the ones his dad always warned him about. Debbie seemed to have more than a friendship in mind, and he'd have to respond one way or the other.

Tentatively, Jonas reached over and took Debbie's hand in his. "So, who else is going to be at this party?" he asked as casually as his racing heart would let him.

"Just some friends," Debbie answered, and Jonas could hear the tremor in her voice too. "It was going to be just some girl-friends of mine, but when you said you'd come, I called a couple of other guys too. My parents don't know that—they think it's just us girls."

"Are you going to get in trouble for having guys there?" Jonas asked somewhat incredulously. Why, Amish guys and girls spent entire weekends together!

"They won't find out. You guys will all be gone by the time they get home."

Hands clasped tightly, Jonas and Debbie talked all the way to her home. "Well, we're here," Debbie said, and Jonas thought he heard reluctance in her voice—the same reluctance with which he gave up her hand.

Debbie had told her friends that if they got to her home while she was gone, they should go on in. When she and Jonas walked into the house, it was alive with teens and music. The party was on.

Some things sure make it different from Amish parties, Jonas thought to himself. For one thing, the lack of alcohol. Here it was, New Year's Eve, and the strongest drink seemed to be a punch spiked with 7-Up. He could imagine what the Amish kids were drinking.

Videos were another difference. Unless they rented a motel room or went to the home of someone who wasn't Amish, he and his friends didn't have access to a TV and VCR. Here, videos seemed to be an important part of the party.

But it wasn't just the obvious differences that Jonas noticed as the evening wore on. The kids were discussing things he knew very little about. High school, the basketball teams, homework they had to do over Christmas vacation, other kids in the church youth group, an upcoming ski trip—none of it had anything to do with his life. The more he heard them talk, the more uneasy he got. What was he doing there anyway? These weren't his people. This wasn't his life. How was he supposed to relate to them if they had nothing in common to talk about?

"Hey, did you guys see David Letterman's anniversary special?" Debbie asked the group lounging around the family room. "It's great! And there's a part I think Jonas will find very interesting! We could watch it and it'd be over right around midnight."

"Yeah, let's!" Tara agreed. "I bet Jonas hasn't ever seen David Letterman. Have you?"

"Guess not," Jonas answered. "My TV needs new batteries, so I haven't been watching much lately."

The group burst out laughing, and Randy, one of the guys, asked, "You really have a battery-powered TV?"

"No, I don't, but some of the guys do," Jonas replied.

"He does have a tape player in his buggy though," Debbie added. "And big speakers. If you ever hear a buggy going down the road blasting Garth Brooks or Mary Chapin Carpenter, that'll be Jonas."

The group laughed again. "I thought you Amish couldn't have that stuff," Randy said. "What's the deal?"

"When they turn 16, they get wild and crazy!" Debbie answered for Jonas, catching his eye and winking. He flushed as their eyes locked.

"Yeah, they take worldly women on out-of-control buggy rides," Tara added, and Jonas's red face darkened at the reminder.

"I think it's time to watch David," Debbie rescued Jonas. "Wait'll you see his Top Ten list."

Debbie slipped the tape into the VCR, and the group settled onto the floor and couches. She sat down next to Jonas, who'd claimed a big pillow and was leaning against it and the sofa.

At first, Jonas wasn't sure why the kids thought David Letterman was so funny. But his interest picked up when David announced the upcoming Top Ten List of Amish pick-up lines. And he laughed as the well-known comedian listed ways to ask out Amish girls.

"He grew up in Indiana," Debbie explained after Dave had finished reading the list. "There must have been an Amish community nearby. What'd you think?"

"It was pretty good," Jonas said. "Not that I know that much about it yet."

"Yet! Did you hear that? He doesn't know much yet, but I bet he'll learn fast!" Randy kidded. "When you get some lines that really work, let me know. I could use a few good ones!"

"And you're assuming the same things will work on us as on Amish girls?" Tara questioned, her voice teasing.

"Okay, let's see," Randy's eyes danced. "We'll make a list of pick-up lines, half for Amish girls and half for 'worldly' girls like Tara and Debbie. Help me out now, Jonas."

Shy though he was, Jonas liked the kids, and felt himself being drawn into their fun and conversation.

"Well, as we all know, worldly girls like our horses and buggies. So how about 'Do you wanna learn to drive my horse?'"

"Yes! That's a great one!" Debbie giggled.

"Here's one for an Amish girl," Randy jumped in. "I have a great CD player in my buggy. You won't believe the sound it puts out!"

Laughing out loud, Jonas looked into Debbie's eyes and said, "Have you ever spun a kitty in a buggy?"

"No, I've had to settle for a runaway," Debbie answered with a grin.

"Oh! I've got another one!" Randy leaped up, pretending to admire something on Tara's head. "That is one cool bonnet—is it new?"

Tara shrieked and doubled over in glee. Catching the spirit, Jonas got to his feet, reached for Debbie's hand, and said as seriously as possible, "Do you barn dance?"

Studying Tara with mock admiration, Randy enthused, "You Amish girls are such seamstresses! Did you make that T-shirt?"

Feeling braver by the second, Jonas pantomimed taking a swig out of a jug. Looking back at Debbie with a wink, he asked, "Would you like to try some of my homemade juice?"

Inspired again, Randy knelt in front of Tara. "You are one hot babe," he paused for dramatic effect. "We aren't related, are we?"

By now the whole group was in stitches, and the sound of

their laughter almost drowned out the chiming of the large grand-father clock in the corner of the family room.

"It's midnight!" Debbie shrieked. "I lost all track of the time!" She scurried into the kitchen and returned a few minutes later with party hats, balloons, pencils, little strips of paper, and string.

"Time to get ready for the new year!" she bubbled. "Take a pencil and paper. Write a New Year's wish on the paper and put it in the balloon. Blow up the balloon and tie it to your ankle with the string. Put on the hat. Then we'll run around stomping each other's balloons. The last person to have their balloon popped gets their wish in the new year!"

Jonas didn't know what to write on his paper. A raise would be nice. Or maybe he'd get his driver's license. And then there was Debbie. As of tonight, there was Debbie. He scribbled something down, slipped the paper in the balloon and blew it up.

With loud whooping and hollering, the teens began chasing each other around the house, trying to step on each other's bal-loons while protecting their own. Jonas's natural agility served him well, and his balloon still bounced behind his ankle when all the others were just bits of plastic on a string.

"You get your wish, Jonas!" Debbie exclaimed. "Now you have to pop the balloon and tell us what it is!"

"You didn't say we'd have to do that," Jonas protested. No way was he going to read what he'd written! Stepping on the bal-loon with the opposite foot, he popped it quickly and picked up the slip of paper. Opening it, he slowly read, "I'd like to get my driver's license." Then he just as quickly stuffed the paper in his shirt pocket.

"Go for it, Jonas!" Tara enthused. "Maybe you can drive a car better than a horse and buggy!" she joked.

"That'd be great!" Debbie added. "Then you could drive yourself to our place," she paused slightly, "to work." Debbie's friends picked up on her obvious pause immediately.

"Hey, did one of those Amish pick-up lines get to you, Debbie?" Randy teased. Nudging Jonas, he continued, "I think it was the one about the homemade juice!'"

"Look, my parents are going to be home soon, and they don't know I invited you guys," Debbie changed the subject. "I'd better get Jonas back to town, and I guess you all will have to clear out too. Leave the mess, I'll clean it up in the morning."

"Yeah, you two better get going so you'll have some time together alone," Randy wouldn't stop. "Happy New Year!"

"Sorry about Randy's teasing," Debbie said as they got into her cold car for the drive back to Star Bowl. "He's a nice guy, but he can be a real pain."

"It's okay," Jonas replied. After a long pause, he added, "I guess he was right—the part about us wanting some time together alone."

"Up until we did the pick-up lines, I was getting the feeling you weren't all that comfortable with the kids there tonight."

"It wasn't anything against them. It's just that I don't know much about the things they're into—you know, sports and high school, videos and all that stuff."

"Yeah, I realized that. And it makes me feel kinda weird. Because I'm somewhere in between. I have my high school world, and the one here on the farm where you and I spend time together. And then you—you have your other world too. You'll probably go to an Amish party tonight yet. You'll probably drink and who knows what else," Debbie's voice suddenly got chilly.

"You make it sound like I shouldn't go," Jonas was surprised. "Why not?"

"Because," Debbie paused. "Just because."

They drove silently until Debbie stopped the car in the Star Bowl parking lot, leaving it running for the warmth.

"What did you really write as your New Year's wish?" she asked, sliding to the middle of the seat, close to Jonas. "I think I'd like to read it," she said, playfully opening his jacket and reaching into his pocket.

Jonas struggled halfheartedly to get away, but he didn't have much room. He soon gave up, and Debbie held the piece of paper in her hand. She flipped on the dome light to see a "D" scrawled on the paper.

"Told you—driver's license," Jonas pointed at the D. His left arm slipped around Debbie's shoulders, and she looked up into his face.

"Is that really what it stands for?" The car's dome light was just enough for her to see his eyes, and she knew his answer before she heard it.

"Guess it could stand for Debbie too."

Debbie reached over to turn the light off, then sat quietly, soaking up his admission. After awhile, she sighed and said, "That's why."

"That's why what?"

"That's why I don't understand you going out to drink and party with the Amish. If we're going together, why would you do that?"

The question sounded loaded—too loaded for the moment.

"I won't," he said. "And you'd better get home before your parents do, and you're not there. There's just one thing," he stopped, hoping to halt the nervousness in his voice. "I may not know much about your kind of parties, but I hear that at midnight on New Year's Eve, people kiss each other. I didn't get mine."

Debbie turned her face toward Jonas. His lips found hers in a short kiss. Faces close, they kissed again. And again. Jonas felt a surge in his body—the same electricity he'd felt earlier when they held hands. He'd kissed girls before, but it had never done this to him. He kissed Debbie one more time softly and longingly. Then, heart beating wildly, he pulled his face away from hers.

"You've gotta go," he whispered huskily.

Chapter 10
The Rest of the Night

Jonas practically floated out of Debbie's warm car and out into the biting Kansas wind. It had been snowing lightly since he'd tied Lightning up at the hitching post hours ago, and his horse blanket sported a soft cover of its own. He untied the twine that held the blanket on, shook the snow off, and laid it on the cold buggy seat. Releasing Lightning's rope from the post, he climbed into the buggy, took the reins in his gloved hands, and pulled the window down in front of him. He grabbed the buffalo hide lap robe he got from his grandparents on his birthday and draped it over his shoulders and legs as much as possible. Jonas turned Lightning away from the post and toward the road. He wouldn't have to guide him the rest of the way home. The horse knew the way.

The snow seemed to be getting heavier as Lightning stepped out onto the road, and Jonas hoped the horse could sense his surroundings better than he could see them. The battery-powered lights on the buggy provided little illumination in the storm. He made sure Lightning was on the paved shoulder and not on the road itself—they didn't need someone to rear-end them due to the poor visibility. Then he sat back for the frigid 40-minute ride home.

Jonas couldn't remember ever being so confused in his life. His attraction to Debbie surprised, scared and excited him. He couldn't deny—he didn't want to forget—the passion in their kisses. But neither could he forget the warnings from his parents, especially the speech from his dad the day they got his new buggy. "Don't date English girls, because what happens if you fall in love?" he could hear his dad clearly. "If you should marry outside the Amish and leave, it would break my heart. Your mother's too."

Is that what was happening? Was he falling in love? No, stupid, he told himself. It was just one evening together, a few kisses. It didn't mean anything.

But he liked her. Her laughter, her bubbly personality, her interest in helping with the farm chores. Not every English girl would want to help with the animals. They had some important things in common. They had fun together. No doubt about it. He liked her a lot.

He couldn't imagine ever telling his parents. He wouldn't.

The buggy stopped. Peering through the snow-covered window, Jonas could barely make out the red sign directly in front of them. Lightning had stopped out of habit. He shook his head once, then turned onto the road toward home and the barn that awaited him.

This storm is serious, Jonas thought, and I'm about as cold as I ever want to be. Maybe if I take a short nap, the time will go faster.

Jonas woke with a start to find himself sliding crazily to his right and down. The buggy was balancing precariously, half on the road shoulder and half in the steep ditch, and Lightning was dancing nervously in front. What in the...?

Jonas half-slid, half-fell out of the buggy and into the ditch. He stumbled through the snow-filled ditch to Lightning, who was getting more panicked by the moment. Soothing him with his voice and hands, he grabbed the bridle so he wouldn't take off. Jonas looked back at the buggy. One of the spokes had broken in a wheel, and the wheel had collapsed. The buggy wasn't going any place without another wheel.

Great, just great, he thought. Stranded in a Kansas blizzard. He'd have to ride Lightning until they found a farm. That, or freeze to death. Or both, he dismayed.

As near as he could figure, they had to be within a mile of someone. No one lived on the mile after the stop sign, but Dan Yoder's were a mile and a half from that intersection. Surely they'd gone a half mile from the stop sign, hadn't they?

The wet snow in the ditch had soaked into his shoes. He hadn't worn a hat that evening, and the stinging wind pushed bullets of snow against his head and face. Quickly he unhitched the useless buggy from the horse and grabbed the lap robe. He took Lightning's bridle off—he'd just hang on and hope Lightning would get them to some shelter. Then he laid the robe on Lightning's back, grabbed his mane, and jumped on the horse. Pulling the robe out from under him, Jonas wrapped it around his head and shoulders the best he could. He bent his head as low as he could, squeezed the horse with his legs, and Lightning began walking.

The possibility of freezing to death in the storm seemed all too real. No one would be looking for him. His parents didn't know where he was and wouldn't expect him home until he showed up. The Amish kids surely wondered why he hadn't come to their party, but they wouldn't be looking for him. Not now. If he got too cold, they'd find him in the morning. Frozen.

It didn't take long before Jonas couldn't feel his feet, hands, or face anymore. They'd gone past the point of hurting. He wondered how long it took for frostbite to happen.

Colder even than the blizzard around him was the fear in Jonas's heart as Lightning pushed his way into the storm. He knew why this had happened. He was being punished—punished by God for getting involved with Debbie. He was supposed to stay Amish, respect his parents and listen to them. Like the snow pelting him now, being with Debbie flew in the face of

God's rules. His sins were finding him out.

He didn't know how much longer he could hold out. Then, ahead of him he could just barely make out an outline of trees— trees surrounding Dan Yoder's farm. He hated to wake them up in the middle of the night, but he would. Yes he would.

When Harlan Schmidt picked Jonas up from his home four hours later to take him to work, Jonas had nothing more to say than a simple "Morning." After awakening Dan and Mattie Yoder, Jonas had accepted their invitation to thaw out and crash by their wood-burning stove for a few hours. He'd put Lightning in their barn—he'd stay there until Jonas could put another buggy wheel on after he was done milking at the Schmidts. Dan had taken him home just in time to meet Harlan coming to get him at 6:00 a.m.

After being nearly frozen and getting very little sleep, Jonas's physical energy was at an all-time low. Emotionally, he felt like he'd been through the wringer in his mother's hand-cranked washing machine. He just wanted to finish his chores, get the buggy and Lightning home, and crash.

Certainly the last thing he wanted to do was see Debbie that morning, and he was glad she must be sleeping in. It meant he had to do the calves alone, and he was so tired, but it beat having to talk to her right then. He was just finishing up with the last row of calves when Debbie came out of the house and headed toward him, stomping playfully in the new snow.

"Wow, we *did* get some snow last night! I love it! It's so pretty!"

"Yep," Jonas acknowledged, rinsing the milk buckets out by the water hydrant.

"It was snowing pretty hard when I drove home. I worried about you," Debbie grew serious.

"Yeah," Jonas grunted.

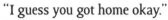

"I guess you got home okay."

"Sorta."

"What do you mean, 'sorta'?"

Jonas let out a long sigh. He didn't want to talk about it. But Debbie hadn't done anything to deserve his rude behavior. So he told her, briefly, what had happened.

"Jonas, that is so scary!" Debbie's eyes widened with concern. "I...I don't know what you'll think about this, but I was praying for you. I was worried, so I prayed you'd get home safely. Thank God you did," she said, touching his arm gently and searching his eyes.

Jonas dropped his gaze. He didn't know what to do with words like that. *She'd* been *praying* for *him?* What was that supposed to mean? Wasn't God punishing him for seeing her? And now she said she'd been praying for him, and was thanking God he got home safely. This was more than he could think about, at least right now.

"Look, Debbie, I'm dead tired. All I want is a bed. Can you take me to Dan Yoder's? I need to borrow a wheel from him, get Lightning, fix the buggy and go home."

"There's something else you should know," Debbie began as she got into the car. Jonas slid into the passenger seat and gave her a tired, questioning look.

"When I got home last night, my parents were here already. They didn't know where I was. I had to tell them that I'd taken you back to town, and that there'd been some other guys here."

"Were they mad?"

"They said they were 'very disappointed' that I didn't tell them the truth at the beginning. They really didn't mind you guys being here. They like you—you know that. But they felt like I was trying to pull something over on them. They didn't like that at all."

"So now what?"

"Since this was the first time I've really messed up, they just said, 'Don't let it happen again'."

The next weekend, when Debbie hinted that they might do something together, Jonas said he was busy. He didn't tell her, but he planned to spend it with the Amish young folks. Where he belonged, he told himself. So far his parents thought he'd been with them on New Year's Eve, and he sincerely hoped it would stay that way.

Other than the morning and evening chores, Harlan had very little work for Jonas during the winter. So Jonas spent more time at home, helping his father work on equipment, cleaning manure out of the barns and cow lots, and repairing buildings they didn't have time to fix during the rest of the year. He enjoyed being with his dad, and as long as he didn't ask too many personal questions about Jonas's life, they got along great.

But Jonas lived in fear of his father finding out about him and Debbie. As the winter wore on, his resolution not to see Debbie had weakened quickly. In fact, within a month of the New Year's Eve party, he'd given in, and was seeing her on the weekends. Debbie's curfew was midnight, however, so Jonas spent the rest of the night with the Amish kids.

He took a lot of flack from the Amish youth about Debbie. "Debbie's Joe," they called him because Debbie drove when they went out on dates. "She must be the boss and he just follows her around," they said. They also accused him of "kissing up to the boss by kissing on his daughter." Jonas tolerated the teasing most of the time, but it was comments from Sue Ann that bothered him the most.

"You really like this girl?" Sue Ann queried Jonas as they played a game of chess at Enos's house the first weekend in March. Enos's family had gone to Illinois for a funeral, which gave him license to invite the young folks to the farm for the weekend. A wild game of cards was going on in the next room, while another group hung around the keg in the barn. The youthful invasion was one that parents dreaded yet half-expected if they left a teenager at home.

"She's okay," Jonas answered Sue Ann noncommittally.

"She must be more than that. You're with her almost every weekend. That's more like going steady," Sue Ann pushed.

"It's not that at all."

"Maybe not yet. But if you keep going with her, it will be. And you might end up having to choose between her and the Amish girls. They're going to start saying that you think you're too good for them."

"Come on, Sue Ann, give me a break! I told you it's not serious!"

"Sorry. I just want you to think about it." Sue Ann contemplated her next move, then said thoughtfully, "Did you know Sam and I broke up last weekend?"

"Yeah, I heard. What happened?"

"He told me he's for sure not going to stay Amish."

"And you are?"

"I think so."

"Why?"

"It's who we are, Jonas. We were born Amish, and that's what we are meant to be. It's all we know."

"You'd give up the guy you love to stay Amish?"

"It's not easy. But maybe it means we aren't supposed to be together."

"What'd Sam say?"

"He wasn't happy about it. But he doesn't want the Amish life. He wants a car, electricity, a phone and TV."

"Those things are sure nice."

"Yeah, you enjoy all of that at Debbie's, don't you?"

"They're there. And I don't see how it makes them any less Christian," Jonas answered almost defensively.

"Maybe it doesn't for them. I guess that's between them and God."

"I guess so," Jonas mumbled. He didn't like these discussions. They always left him confused.

Jonas knew Debbie didn't like him hanging out with the Amish kids after he left her at midnight. He assured her that he didn't like any of the girls the way he cared for her, and that seemed to help a bit. Still, he detected more than a little jealousy and questioning in her voice when she asked, one Friday evening on their way to a movie, "So, what's happening after midnight tonight? Who gets to spend the rest of the night with you?"

Jonas's eyes questioned hers, and she responded, "That is, if you don't mind telling me."

"I don't mind. There'll probably be a bunch of kids at Sam's apartment watching videos. I'll go there."

"Sam has his own apartment?"

"He got it about a month ago. He says he's not going back to the Amish."

"So you all hang out there a lot?"

"Uh huh."

After a few moments, Debbie turned a flirtatious smile on Jonas and asked, "Would you spend the night with me if I asked you to?"

Knowing there had to be something more behind the question, Jonas decided to play it to the hilt. He slid over close to Debbie, put his arm around her and whispered, "Just say when, and where."

Debbie giggled and pretended embarrassment. "You'll be disappointed. I'm serious about the invitation. It's just that we'll be at the YMCA with my whole church youth group."

"Say more."

"Well, we're having a lock-in next Saturday. We start with a pizza supper, then our leaders do a session on God or something, and then we spend the rest of the night playing sports, watching videos, eating, hanging out. We can bring friends, and I thought you might want to come. The kids that were at the New Year's Eve party will be there, plus others."

"I'd have to give up my night with the young folks," Jonas was teasing now.

"A major sacrifice, I know."

"I think I could manage. Just for you, of course," he tightened his arm around her shoulders. "Sounds good to me."

The next Saturday Jonas found himself in a group of 30 teenagers and their adult leaders at the Wellsford YMCA. He was glad he knew a few of them already, and that Debbie stuck pretty close to him. He wasn't big on talking to people he didn't know.

After supper, the group sat down on cushions in one of the meeting rooms. "It's kind of like Sunday school, only better," Debbie explained to Jonas.

That's a big help, he thought to himself. Amish churches don't have Sunday school, so I still don't know what I'm in for here.

"We're going to be talking about 'Who is God?'" announced a short, stocky male leader who stood in front of the group. "I want each of you to think of a kind of car that describes how you see God. Then we'll go around the group and hear your descriptions."

God? Like a *car*? Jonas threw Debbie a "what did you get me into?" look. She just shrugged.

He didn't even know much about cars. Sam had a Camero. Debbie drove a Plymouth Horizon. Enos had that old Honda until he wrecked it, and now he had a Mustang. Was God like any of those, and if so, how?

The group began sharing their cars and how they symbolized God. The closer it came to Jonas's turn, the more nervous he got. What was he going to say? How could he compare God to a car when having a car was against the Amish religion?

"Jonas, we're glad you're with us tonight," the leader said. "What kind of car does God seem like to you?"

"A police car, I guess," Jonas heard his voice shaking.

"A police car. Okay, and why is that?"

"Because it comes after you when you do something wrong."

The group laughed lightly, and the leader smiled. "Thanks, Jonas. Debbie?"

"I see God as a big van, where there's room for a lot of people, and you can always squeeze one more in. And since it's God, you don't have to worry about seat belts for everyone!"

"That's a wonderful picture of God!" the leader complimented. "Okay, let's see what the Bible says about God."

Following the leader's instructions, the group spent the next hour looking up Bible passages and talking about the character of God. Jonas didn't know what to make of what he was hearing. God was being portrayed as a loving parent, a friend, someone who yearned to communicate with people. Either he hadn't been listening to the preachers (and Jonas knew that was a strong possibility), or the Amish picture of God was quite different from that of Debbie and her church. He was glad when the session was over.

The rest of the night was much better, and Jonas enjoyed the games and videos. He was even starting to feel comfortable around the other kids. Tired, yet energized from being together, Jonas and Debbie sat close as they drove back to the farm at daybreak. They were getting pretty good at holding hands while driving, with Jonas using his free right hand to shift the manual transmission.

"You're learning how to drive," Debbie joked. "Maybe you

can get your New Year's wish after all—you know, your driver's license," she nudged him. "I'm sure my dad would teach you and take you in to do the test."

94

"Yeah, and my dad would have a fit."

Chapter
10

Chapter 11

Runaway Buggy

"I can't believe you really did it," Fred Bontrager glared at his son across the supper table. "The minute I saw you in Wellsford with Harlan, I knew what was up. I knew he'd brought you in to get your license."

"It's just so I can drive the truck to help him farm, and to drive back and forth to work," Jonas's voice challenged the anger in his father's. "I can do the work of any man around the farm, but when it comes to driving, I'm like a little boy. I can't haul wheat during harvest, or run to town for parts or feed, or anything. And I hate having to depend on them to pick me up and take me home."

"Yeah, he hates to ride with Debbie," Jonas's younger brother Robert taunted. "He hates it so much!"

"Quiet, Robert," Fred focused the glare on his youngest son. "This is between me and Jonas."

"Not much between him and Debbie when they go driving together," Robert's twin sister Rebecca whispered to him. They both giggled quietly behind their hands.

"Children, time to clear the table and wash the dishes," Esther instructed her family. "Let's do our prayer."

Eight chairs clattered as they were pushed back from the table, and the Bontrager family knelt beside their chairs for the traditional after-meal prayer. The German prayer they recited flowed automatically out of each mouth. Jonas's mouth repeated the communication with God, but his mind wrestled with his father. He knew his dad would be mad about the license, but it was a risk he was willing to take. He just hoped Fred had said what he needed to say, and would leave it at that.

No sooner had the "Amen" been muttered by the family than Jonas found himself being attacked from four directions by his siblings. "Under the table! Under the table!" they chanted, pulling him down from where he still knelt beside his chair. "Under the table, birthday boy!"

Jonas laughed as he willingly took his place under the dining room table. He'd been almost afraid that his family had forgotten his 17th birthday. Nobody had said anything about it to him when he got home from work, so he'd thought there'd be a big surprise birthday party at supper. When none of the relatives showed up for supper, he told himself he wasn't disappointed. But he was. Then the supper table discussion turned to focus on his driver's license. It hadn't been the best of birthdays. At least not at home.

Debbie's family was a different story, he thought wryly. Debbie had greeted him with a big card and a birthday kiss, right in the middle of the farmyard. Embarrassed, Jonas didn't know how to react, but it felt good anyway. Then at lunch Harlan and his wife, Lynne, had invited him to eat with them—even though Debbie was in school. Lynne had made his favorite meal—he'd eaten there enough that she knew he loved her smothered steak—and topped it off with birthday cake and ice cream. He certainly felt loved and appreciated in the Schmidt family.

Jonas's thoughts returned to the present, and the fact that he was still sitting under the dining room table. As he crawled out, he heard the sound of buggy wheels outside the house, and looked questioningly at his mother.

"Well, who could that be?" she feigned surprise.

No, his family hadn't forgotten. A number of his relatives had gone to a consignment sale that evening, so Jonas's mother had invited everyone over for homemade ice cream after the sale. Soon the house hummed with the chatter of men outside on the porch, the women in the kitchen, and children everywhere.

"Irvin P. just came back from Gainesboro," one of Jonas's uncles said to the men eating ice cream. "Said some of them down there are talkin' about going from steel wheels to air tires on their tractors."

"I can't believe it!" Fred exclaimed, and Jonas looked up to see the same anger in his father's eyes he'd seen just an hour earlier. "We still farm with horses. It was bad enough when they went to tractors years ago. Now they're going to air tires!?"

"It's mostly the Schrock brothers, I think," the uncle continued. "They say it's so hard on their equipment, rattling down the road like that on steel wheels."

"Should've stayed with horses in the first place," Fred muttered, scraping the bottom of his ice cream bowl. "Just goes to show what happens when you start giving in. One year it's tractors. Then air tires. Next they'll be putting cabs on the tractors and taking the family to town in them. I've heard that's happening in Oklahoma."

"Well, right now it's just talk. Fact is, Irvin said the guy who told him didn't really want it talked around. Sounds bad to me though."

Jonas usually was so tired, he fell asleep soon after crawling into bed. But the evening of his 17th birthday, he lay awake thinking about the day, and wondering.

Why was it so wrong, in his dad's eyes, for him to drive? Why couldn't his father see the logical reasons behind him getting his license? And why had his dad reacted so negatively to the news that people in another Amish community in Kansas were talking about getting air tires on their tractors? Why, for that matter, was his community still using horses for farming? Did using horses, or steel wheels, really make them better or closer to God?

He wasn't sure how. Because when he looked at the Schmidt family, they seemed pretty religious too. Only in a different way. They talked more about God, and not as much about traditional things in their religion, things that "we've always done this way."

Debbie was very open about her religion. He still didn't know what to think about her praying for him back on New Year's Eve, and how she thought God had answered her prayer. They hadn't talked about it since—maybe Debbie could sense he was uncomfortable with the topic. He hadn't gone back with her to her youth group either, even though she kept asking him. Once was enough.

Fact was, Jonas realized, he didn't know what he believed or where he fit in right now. He didn't like his dad's strict attitude, but he hated the thought of not getting along with his father. Just a year ago today they'd made that trip into Wellsford together to buy his buggy, and that evening Dad had given him Lightning. He'd really liked his dad then. But now he seemed to be angry and frustrated too much of the time.

On the other hand, he got along great with the Schmidts, and he liked them. But all that God-talk made him uneasy, and sometimes he wished they'd be more quiet about their religion.

Maybe the only group he really felt he belonged in was the Amish young folks. They just hung out, had fun, and didn't worry about much. Like Enos kept saying, "You're only young once," and then he'd go off and do something crazy or stupid.

No, that wasn't really him either, Jonas concluded. He didn't want to live just for the moment. It's just that he didn't know *how* he wanted to live his moments, now or in the future.

His mind still turning, Jonas finally fell asleep.

"Finally, *I* get to drive *you* someplace," Jonas opened the door for Debbie to get into her car, and then walked around to take his place behind the wheel. "Where do you want to go?"

"Oh, any place safe," Debbie snuggled close to him. "Last time I was with you and you drove, we had a little…"

"Yeah, yeah, yeah, I know. You'll never let me forget that, will you?"

"Just kidding, Jonas. I don't care where we go—just for a drive in the country."

So they drove, slowly at first while Jonas gained confidence, loving the feel of the car under him and Debbie beside him.

He must not have been paying attention, because suddenly Jonas found himself approaching his parents' farm. He hadn't meant to go there. He didn't want them to see him. Yet he seemed unable to do anything but continue along the road, hoping no one would notice him. Then, without warning, his father ran out of the driveway and onto the road, not even looking right or left, but waving his arms frantically. Instinctively, Jonas hit the brakes. The car skidded on the sand road, and Jonas desperately cranked the wheel to miss his father. He heard a thud as the car swerved into the deep ditch, rolled over and came to rest on its wheels. Debbie suddenly forgotten, Jonas jumped out and ran to the still form of his father lying on the road. Then he ran toward his house, screaming.

Jonas woke when he felt himself starting to scream.

His eyes flicked open and he recognized the familiar ceiling. A dream, all a horrible dream.

The dream stayed in the back of Jonas's mind all the next day. He couldn't shake the horror of hitting his father, of the guilt that it happened while he was driving, that if his father had died, he would never have forgiven himself. And every time he reminded himself it was just a dream, he realized the situations that stimulated the dream were real. Very, very real.

A week later, Debbie asked Jonas to go to the prom with her. And before he could say no or make excuses, she explained that her family wanted to buy him a suit to wear "because you should have a nice suit and because it's a little bonus for being such good help," Debbie quoted her mother. Jonas had a lot of hesitations, but none of them seemed strong enough to argue about with Debbie. Obviously she and her family wanted him to escort her. So he agreed. On one condition. That the suit would be kept at Debbie's house, and he would get ready there for the evening out. No point in feeding his father's anger or mistrust any further.

The Wednesday before the Saturday prom, the Bontrager family received word that Esther's aunt in Illinois had died of cancer. Fred and Esther made plans to join a van load of Amish people traveling to the Illinois Amish community for the funeral.

"Jonas and Roseanne are in charge of the rest of you and seeing that the chores get done. You'll all have to pitch in and help, and behave yourselves," Fred said that evening as the family gathered for supper. "I expect you to stay around here this weekend," he addressed Jonas. "Understand?"

"Yeah, I understand," Jonas answered, thinking to himself, *I understand. What you don't understand is that I have a life too.*

Knowing he couldn't trust his younger siblings, Jonas told Roseanne Saturday morning about his plans for the evening, and swore her to secrecy. Although she didn't tell the younger kids where he went, they all knew Jonas left that evening with his horse and buggy. That's all they needed for ammunition when Fred and Esther returned Sunday evening.

"Jonas left Saturday evening," 12-year-old Orie announced moments after Fred and Esther entered the house.

"Okay, we'll talk about it later," Fred threw a glance at Jonas. "Everything else go okay?"

"Yeah, we did fine," 13-year-old David answered. "You can go away any time. We even got used to Roseanne's cooking."

"But we're glad you're home, Mommy," Rebecca reached for her mother's hand.

"Yeah, me too," Robert added.

"Jonas." Fred's voice came from behind the paper he was reading just as his son opened the door to go upstairs. The school kids were in bed, and Jonas had hoped he could slip up to his bedroom before Fred caught him, but it hadn't worked out that way.

"Yes?"

"Come tell me where you went Saturday night."

Jonas slumped onto the couch next to his father's recliner. Esther came from the kitchen and sat down in the rocker beside Fred.

Jonas took a deep breath and started, his head bowed, eyes on the floor. "Awhile back, Debbie asked me to go to the prom with her. I said I would. It's a big deal for high school kids, and it was Saturday night. I couldn't break my promise and back out. It wouldn't be right to break my promise," he finished, finally looking up at his parents. "Would it?"

Fred studied Jonas's face for what seemed like a long time to his 17-year-old son.

"It's not the promise I'm worried about. It's why you said yes in the first place. Why did you agree to go with her?"

"I don't know."

"This prom thing. Don't you need really nice clothes? What did you wear?" Esther queried.

"The Schmidt's bought me a suit."

"The Schmidt's bought you a suit!" Jonas heard the anger rising in Fred's voice. "Harlan helps you get your license. They buy you a suit. They encourage you to date their daughter. I'm getting the feeling they'd just as soon have you in their family!"

"Fred..." Esther reached out to touch her husband's arm.

"No, I'm not done yet," Fred leaned forward, his face close to his son's. "A year ago, on your 16th birthday, I told you what can happen if you start dating English girls. I didn't dream you would go against us so soon. You're heading down the wrong road, Jonas," Fred paused, and when he continued, the tone in his voice seemed to have changed from anger to deep hurt and sadness. "You're like a runaway buggy. What scares me is that the worldly 'horse' pulling you doesn't know her way home like Amish horses do. At least not to the home where you belong."

Chapter 12

Fireworks

"I heard you were in church last Sunday," Enos teased Jonas as they changed the oil in Enos's Mustang a week after the prom. "Mom and Dad said they saw you there. You thinking about joining or something?"

"No way. My folks made me go."

"Since when do your parents make you go? You haven't been to church since you turned 16. None of us have! We ain't going 'til we're ready to join! If we ever do!" Enos laughed. "Tell you what, that's a long way off for me."

"They made me go because I went to the prom with Debbie."

"What? How'd they find out?"

"I had to tell them because I was supposed to stay home that weekend. The folks were gone to a funeral in Illinois."

"Oh. I still don't know why they made you go to church."

"They said that if I liked to dress up so much, it was time I put on my Sunday clothes for a change. Plus, church was at my uncle's. I thought it'd be easier to go than fight them about it."

"You must have felt stupid, being the only one there."

"Yeah, me and the guys and girls who're gonna join and get married—we were the only young folks. Everybody wondered why I was there. They thought I was joining. They kept saying they didn't know I was going steady with a girl."

"You're going steady all right—and that's why you were in church—because she's not Amish."

"I am not going steady."

"Yeah, right."

"Look, Enos, I'm not. And I wish everybody would quit saying that."

"Only way they'll quit is if you don't spend so much time with her."

Jonas thought about what Enos said. He didn't want to quit seeing Debbie, but he didn't like the way people had them matched for life. He was thinking about how to raise the issue with Debbie when she helped solve the problem for him.

"I got a job for the summer," she said one morning late in May as they fed the calves together. "I'm going to work at the Pizza Hut. Evenings and a lot of weekends. I hate that because we can't do stuff together, but I had to take what I could get."

"That's okay. We can still see each other during the day, here on the farm."

"It isn't the most romantic setting in the world." Debbie set down the bucket she was carrying and reached out to stop Jonas, who was walking beside her. She took his hands and stood facing him. "But it'll have to be good enough."

Jonas scanned the yard quickly to see if anyone was around, then quickly kissed Debbie on the mouth. "It'll be okay," he said, putting his arm around her waist. They picked up their milk buckets and walked towards the barn.

June flew by for Jonas. Long hours at work intermingled with stolen moments with Debbie kept him busy and happy during the weeks, and weekend nights he spent with the Amish young folks. A group of the guys, including Jonas and Enos, had decided to play on a city league baseball team, so that took a lot of their time too. One evening late in June, after a game, one of the non-Amish players named Paul asked Enos what the Amish kids were doing on the 4th of July.

"Having a party, I imagine," Enos answered with a grin. "Don't take much of an excuse to have a party, and 4th of July sounds like a good one to me."

"You ever been to see the fireworks in Vicksburg?" Paul asked.

"Nope. Something we should see?"

"It's pretty cool. You should check it out, and then go have your party."

"I suppose we could do that. Can't say I'd know my way around Vicksburg though. Where are the fireworks? How'd we get there?"

"It's easy. Right off of the interstate. Just don't take the wrong exit and end up in the bad part of the town. Gangbangers might want that hot car of yours," Paul nodded toward Enos's '68 Mustang. "And you don't argue with them guys."

"Aw, nobody's gonna bother my car. They want the new ones. Fact is, I wouldn't mind cruisin' down one of those streets. I've always wondered what these gangs look like."

"They'd be lookin' at *you*, Enos, and you'd stick out like a sore thumb," Paul warned. "That would be just plain stupid. Looks like I'm going to have to make sure you don't get yourself killed in Vicksburg. How about if you all ride with us, and then we'll go to your party afterwards?"

Enos looked around at the other Amish guys and girls who'd been listening to the conversation. "Shall we go see some fireworks and then introduce these dudes to a river party?"

The "sure's!" sealed the deal.

"Have cooler, will party!" Enos yelled as he jumped out of his Mustang at the ball diamond the evening of July 4. "Where do I put this sucker? Who's driving?"

"I am. Here!" Paul opened the trunk of his car. "Add it to the collection."

Enos sandwiched his cooler in among the others, then opened it and took out a soda. "Packed it so we can take it in at the fireworks. They probably have some stupid rule about alcohol, don't they?"

"Yeah, they do," Paul agreed. "We'll refill the coolers on our way to the river."

Jonas heard the conversation as he came up to the car. At least they wouldn't have any beer before driving to Vicksburg and in the city itself.

By the time they arrived at the Vicksburg College stadium an hour later, the long Kansas summer evening had turned to dusk. The two cars of young people from the Wellsford community joined the lines of cars waiting to park, and then the dozen kids followed the crowd making its way to the stadium.

"Can you believe all these people?" Jonas fell in step alongside Sue Ann.

"Yeah, I know. Sam and I came here once to see a football game. It was just like this then."

"You came to Vicksburg to see a football game?"

"Sure, why not?"

"I just didn't know many of the young folks came to Vicksburg."

"They don't. But Sam's always been different. He wasn't afraid of the city. In fact, I wouldn't be surprised if he ends up living in one someday."

"Well, it's not for me. Too many cars and people I don't trust. You should have heard my parents when they found out we're going to Vicksburg. Mom had a fit 'cause she'd just read in the paper about somebody being killed by a gang member here in the city."

"Yeah, I read that too," Sue Ann said. "I guess it's kinda scary. But don't they just shoot each other? Why should we be worried?"

"I guess we shouldn't. It'll be fun to see the fireworks, but then I'll be ready to get out of town."

"Me too."

Jonas had to admit, the fireworks show was great. He didn't understand how the music and fireworks could be choreographed so perfectly together, and when they played the "Star Spangled Banner" at the end with an incredible light show, he felt chills up and down his spine. He wished Debbie could see this with him. Oh well, she'd probably seen it before, he reasoned. She'd seen and done a lot of things he was experiencing for the first time.

After the show ended, Enos and some of the other guys took off running for the cars, thinking they'd be able to beat the traffic rush out of the parking lot. "Walk along the sidewalk, and we'll drive by and pick you up," Enos yelled back at Jonas, Sue Ann and the others walking behind. "Bring my cooler!"

Jonas looked at the cooler between him and Sue Ann and laughed. "Now he tells us," he said.

Jonas and the group of walkers were nearing the parking lot when they heard fireworks coming from that direction, followed immediately by terrified screams. Jonas and Sue Ann looked at each other, then ahead. They could see people crouching behind cars, and several men appeared to be wrestling someone to the ground. Nearby, a group was gathering around a person lying on the concrete. One of the bent figures stood up, and Jonas recognized Paul.

"That's our guys!" Jonas yelled at Sue Ann, dropping the cooler and breaking into a run. Reaching them within seconds, Jonas cried out when he recognized the still form on the ground.

"Enos! Enos! What happened?"

Jonas knelt at Enos's head, half-noticing the blood pooling around his knees. He clasped Enos's bloody face in his hands and begged, "Enos, stay with me, man! You'll be okay! Hang on, buddy! We're getting help!"

Enos opened his mouth, and Jonas bent low to hear him. But the only thing that came out was a slow trickle of blood.

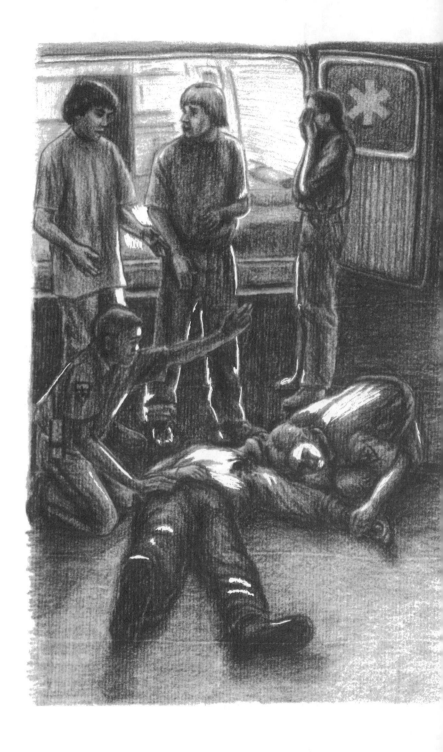

It seemed an eternity that Jonas and the other Amish kids crouched around Enos, talking to and encouraging him while the sound of sirens grew closer. With every heartbeat, blood spurted from a gaping hole in Enos's neck. Sue Ann tried to cover it, to apply pressure to stop the flow, but the wound was too big. Finally the ambulance screamed into the parking lot. The sirens stopped, and two EMT's came running toward the group.

"Please, please stand back!"

Jonas forced himself to stand up and move away, never taking his eyes off his fallen friend. He watched in disbelief as one of the EMT's leaned down to check Enos's breathing and listen to his chest. She felt for a pulse, then looked at the other EMT kneeling beside her and said, "We've gotta start CPR."

No! Jonas screamed inside. He can't die! No! No! No!

Within moments, medics arrived with a stretcher. They hurriedly lifted Enos onto it, and just as quickly pushed the stretcher into the ambulance. Sirens wailing, strobe lights flashing, the white emergency vehicle rolled out of the parking lot and onto the street.

"Were you with that young man?" a police officer asked the group of stunned teens.

"Yes!" Jonas answered. "How do we get to the hospital?"

"If you get in your cars, I'll escort you there," the officer said.

"I'm sorry." The blue-gowned, blood-flecked doctor addressed the quiet group of Amish teens in the lobby of Vicksburg Hospital's emergency room. "There was nothing we could do. The bullet hit the major artery in his neck. He'd lost too much blood by the time he got here. He went into shock. We couldn't get him back. I'm so sorry."

"What happened?" Jonas's voice shook. "Who shot Enos? Why?"

"If you'll come with me to the waiting room, I need to talk to all of you," the police officer answered. "I need to get some information on your friend. We need to call his family. And I'll tell you what we know so far about the shooting."

Numbly, the young people moved to the waiting room and sat down. Some sobbed audibly, some quietly, and others seemed too shocked to cry. Jonas tried to focus on the questions the police officer was asking him.

"Your name?"

"Jonas Bontrager."

"And the young man who was shot?"

"Enos Miller."

"His parents?"

"David and Katie Miller."

"Address?"

"They live outside of Wellsford."

"Phone?"

"They don't have one. They're Amish."

The officer looked at Jonas and the other young people. "You all Amish?"

They nodded.

"You don't *look* Amish. I mean, your clothes."

The last thing Jonas wanted to do was explain why Amish teens wore English clothes.

"Believe me, sir, we're Amish. You'll have to call one of the neighbors and have them go tell David and Katie."

"I'll probably call the local sheriff and ask him to go see them," the officer said.

After making the call, the officer turned to the group and said, "We don't know a lot right now about who shot Enos, but we're quite certain it was gang-related. From what witnesses said, some rival gang members began throwing their signs at each other in the parking lot. Each gang has its own hand signal, and when they start signaling at each other, or throwing their signs, it's a challenge. One thing led to another, guns were pulled, and Enos happened to get caught in crossfire between them."

"Did you catch the guy who did it?" Jonas was angry now. "Does he know he killed an innocent person?"

"We do have someone in custody, but that's all I can tell you right now."

Jonas buried his head in his hands, anger and hurt tearing at his soul. Why, Why, Why? Enos didn't deserve to die.

Did he? Was this the result of disobeying his parents and God? Had his reckless life caught up with him? That verse, the one the bishop used so often... "the wages of sin is death." Is this what he meant?

Chapter 13

The Viewing

Black buggies began rolling into the farmyard of David and Katie Miller long before dawn and continued all day on July 5, joining the half dozen that had already been there all night. Stopping at the house, the sweaty horses waited while women and children stepped out of the buggies and walked silently into the house, carrying boxes and baskets of food. Then, under the quiet signals of the driver, the horses pulled up alongside the growing line tied up along the fence row. The men and older boys got out of the buggies and strode toward the large white barn in the middle of the yard.

It was time to support a grieving family, and to prepare for a funeral.

While the men took care of milking the cows and feeding David Miller's livestock, the women divided up into different rooms to begin the meticulous housecleaning that always preceded a family having church in their home. A family usually had several months to prepare for church. The Miller home needed to be ready for a funeral in several days.

Jonas hadn't slept at all that night, and neither had he told the Schmidts that he wouldn't be at work. They'd know not to expect him—that he would be helping at the Millers. As he methodically slipped a milker onto one of the Miller's big Holstein dairy cows, he glanced at his father working with the cow in the row across from him.

Fred looked up in time to catch Jonas's eye. "Enos won't ever milk these cows again."

"I know."

"Or work with David on anything."

"I know."

"It's a shame. A young life wasted."

"I know."

"Maybe it will be a lesson for you all."

"It wasn't his fault, Dad. It wasn't his fault he got shot."

Fred finished putting the milker on his cow and moved on to the next one. Jonas paralleled his father's movements in his row of cows.

"Getting shot wasn't his fault. But you and I both know Enos was being wild before it happened."

"Yeah," Jonas muttered. He didn't have the physical or emotional energy to argue with his father. Even if he tried, he didn't know if he'd believe his own arguments.

"We never know when it'll be our time to go. We have to be ready any time," Fred added. "It's too bad Enos hadn't been baptized and joined the church."

A slow stream of buggies came and went from the Miller farm that day. Some people brought condolences and food. Men arrived to help with the field work—this was a busy time of year and the farming had to go on. Jonas stayed around the yard and house all day, helping where he could. Sue Ann and some of the other young folks that had gone to the fireworks were there too. They found themselves repeating the events of the prior evening over and over as new people arrived who were curious about the circumstances surrounding Enos's death.

Around noon, a car drove into the yard. It stopped, and a young woman got out. She approached the small group of young folks eating lunch outside on the picnic table.

"Is this the home of David and Katie Miller?"

"Yes," Jonas answered.

"Do you know where I could find some of the young people

Enos was with last night?"

The teenagers exchanged glances, but no one spoke. Finally, Jonas acknowledged, "We were there."

"Oh! Good! I mean, I'm sorry to hear about what happened to your friend. But I was wondering if I could talk to you a little bit."

Jonas shrugged, and the reporter continued.

"Can you tell me, is it normal for Amish teenagers to go to Vicksburg for the fireworks? Weren't you pretty far from home? How'd you get there?"

"We went with some friends," Jonas answered.

"Did your parents know you were going?"

"What difference does it make?" Jonas replied.

"Well, I just thought it was unusual for you all to be there."

No one answered.

"Were you with Enos when the shooting happened?" the reporter tried a different approach.

"We were a little ways behind him."

"Did you know there were gang members in the parking lot?"

"No."

"Would you recognize them if you saw some?"

"Probably not."

"Do you think Enos knew what happened?"

"Probably not."

"What are your parents saying about all of this?"

No one answered.

"Okay, just one more question. Do you know when the funeral will be?"

"No, not yet."

"Okay, thanks. Thanks for your time."

The reporter walked back and got into her car. After driving to the end of the lane, she stopped, got out with a camera, and took pictures of the line of horses and buggies tied up along the fence.

Jonas and the other young people spent the hot July afternoon getting the farm ready for the funeral. Jonas got the push mower out of the shed and began mowing the grass, Sue Ann cleaned the outdoor toilet and weeded the flower beds, and several of the youth washed the house's windows. They were taking a tea break at the picnic table when a long black car turned slowly into the Miller yard. The hearse stopped near the house, and two men got out. David Miller met them at the door.

Although Jonas couldn't hear the words in the low tones of the men's voices, he knew what was being said. The hearse contained Enos's body, and the men were asking if the coffin was ready. David motioned toward the barn from which hammering sounds had been coming all afternoon. Levi Petersheim, the Amish man who took care of the community's funeral needs, had arrived late in the morning with new pine boards, and by now, his work should be almost completed.

David stepped out of the house and motioned listlessly to Jonas and the three other young men to join him. Shoulders sagging, he led them towards the barn.

"The undertakers are here," David said without looking at the man just inside the barn door. His eyes seemed pulled toward the new pine box resting on two sawhorses. "They're ready for the coffin."

"It's done," Levi answered. "I'm just finishing up the lid."

Jonas and his friends each picked up a corner of the lightweight coffin and carried it to the house. Once inside, they set it down in a bedroom that had been cleaned out and would be used as a viewing room until the funeral. Without air-conditioning or even electric fans to move the air around, the house was very hot, and Jonas was glad to get back outside. He was glad the funeral would be held in the large machine shed. It might not be quite as stifling hot out there.

Sunset brought little relief to the Amish gathered at the

Miller home just 24 hours after the shooting. The south wind that had blown all day had died down, and the air hung heavy with humidity. Tired, hot, and racked with grief he didn't show, Jonas dreaded the singing that evening.

He remembered his first singing—the one when Sam's brother Sol showed up drunk, driving that beat-up old Honda. The Honda that Enos bought from Sol at a river party. Crazy Enos. Crazy, wild, happy Enos. And now...now Enos was dead and they had to sing for him.

The young people clumped together outside, talking in low voices, until the front door opened and one of the Amish ministers motioned them in. Jonas and Sue Ann happened to be standing together, and when his eyebrows raised the silent question, she nodded. They walked in together and joined the others filling in the long rows of gray church benches in the living room.

When everyone was seated and holding songbooks, Sue Ann led them in the first song. Amidst muffled sobs and breaking voices, the group sang for about an hour. Just when Jonas felt he'd die if he couldn't get a breath of fresh air, the minister stood up to thank the young people for singing, and announced that the funeral would be Thursday at 10:00.

"Viewing of the body is anytime between now and then," he said.

After taking a break outside, Jonas went back in. All day he'd been dreading what was coming next. He would have to look at Enos. He would have to confront the horrible hole in his neck. He would have to stare at the lifeless body of his best friend. Head down and hands in his pockets, he forced himself toward the bedroom where Enos's body lay.

I've never seen him so quiet, Jonas thought to himself, studying the body before him. He was always so full of life and fun. The wound—it doesn't look so bad. Guess the undertaker and makeup can fix a lot of things.

Jonas gazed down at Enos, half-expecting him to breathe, his chest to move up and down. The plain white shirt and dark navy buttonless jacket remained motionless. The legs that the evening before had run past Jonas—now unnaturally still in dark navy barn-door pants. The laughing voice that reminded Jonas to bring his cooler—now silent. Jonas wanted to sob, to cry out, to scream, but he couldn't. He could only stand and stare.

"Amish Teen Is Gang Victim" the newspaper heading bombarded Jonas when he went to get the family mail the next morning. Stopping in the middle of the lane, he read:

> *An 18-year-old rural Wellsford man, Enos Miller, was shot and killed Monday evening near the Vicksburg College stadium as he was running through the parking lot following the fireworks. According to Vicksburg's Chief of Police Len Stroudman, gunshots were apparently being exchanged between rival gang members in the parking lot outside of the stadium.*
>
> *"The young man simply got caught in between," Stroudman said.*
>
> *Miller, whose parents, David and Katie Miller, are Amish, was in Vicksburg with a number of other Amish young people when the incident happened. The Amish are well-known for their simple lifestyle and efforts to remain apart from "the world." Ironically, this shooting incident has brought them into tragic contact with a violent world.*

Jonas folded the paper back and trudged toward the house.

"What's gonna happen to his car?" Lavern Yoder asked,

sweat dripping from his darkly tanned face. He tossed his shovel on the ground and picked up the red water jug.

"Who knows? Is it still at the ball diamond?" Jonas wondered, his shirt clinging to his back. He bent down toward the hole in the ground and shoveled out a scoop full of dirt. "I'll take that jug when you're done with it."

"It must be, but they'll tow it before long. Where do you suppose the keys are?"

"Enos had them. Which means...I guess it means David and Katie got them along with his clothes."

"You guys want some water?" Jonas asked the other two teens digging the grave in the Amish cemetery.

"Thanks," one of them said, pausing for a long drink. "We should've done this early this morning, or late tonight, anytime but during the day."

"I don't know why they can't hire a guy to do this with a backhoe, like everybody else does," the other digger added.

"Because it's always been done this way," Lavern answered.

"I don't mind," Jonas said. "It's the last thing we can do for Enos."

Chapter 14

Funeral

Jonas was awakened at 4:30 the next morning so he could do his father's share of the morning chores. Along with four other men, Fred had spent the night sitting with the body, and he needed to catch a few hours of sleep before the family left for the funeral. Amish tradition called for someone to be with the body at all times up until the funeral, and Levi Petersheim had arranged volunteers into shifts around the clock.

After chores and breakfast, the family got ready and left for the Miller home in their horse and buggy. From miles around, horses and buggies were converging on the farmstead. One after the other, they rattled into the yard. Jonas was driving the family surrey packed with his parents and five siblings. As a pallbearer, he had been asked to provide the buggy that he and the five other teenage pallbearers would take from the farm to the cemetery. They would be the first to leave the yard, preceding the hearse buggy.

As he stepped out of the buggy and unhitched the family driving mare, Jonas noticed several vans parked around the yard. People had come from other communities, even other states. The Oklahoma young folks would probably be here, including Will, whose horse had died when Enos's car hit it.

No sooner had the thought crossed his mind than Jonas spotted the Oklahoma group, clustered together under the big elm tree in the middle of the yard. Several of the Wellsford young people had joined them, including Sue Ann. After tying the mare to the fence, Jonas walked slowly toward the group, getting there in time to hear Sue Ann say, "No, he didn't say anything. But you should've seen the look in his eyes."

"How'd he look?" Jonas recognized Will as the speaker.

"Scared. Terribly, terribly scared."

"Scared to die, I bet he was."

"Well, who wouldn't be?"

"Did he know he was dying? Did *you* know?" Will questioned.

"I think he knew. I…I was trying to stop the bleeding. There was so much blood, and it wouldn't stop. I kept hoping…" Sue Ann's voice trailed off and broke into a sob.

People began moving toward the shed and filing into the rows and rows of backless church benches. When everyone was inside and standing, Jonas and the other five somber young pallbearers took their places near the front, followed by Enos's family—his mother Katie, leaning heavily on her husband's shoulder; his brothers and sisters, seemingly in a daze; two sets of elderly grandparents; and rows of aunts and uncles and cousins. Finally the procession stopped, and a minister told the people to be seated.

"Song number 23," the *Vorsinger* (song leader) stood up and announced. "And Fred Bontrager, will you lead?"

Jonas couldn't see his father, but his heart skipped a beat and then began racing. Poor Dad, he thought. Of all the times to be asked to lead—today, at a funeral, when there's all these other people here. He heard his father's clear tenor voice lead out in the first syllable, moving through three notes for just that syllable. Jonas had heard a CD with Gregorian chants on it at Debbie's house, and if you stretched your imagination a bit, they might be compared to Amish songs. But not really, he thought, joining the a cappella singsong chanting around him.

After the first song, the *Vorsinger* announced another one, calling on another man in the congregation to lead it. This process continued for four songs, then one of the ministers stood up to preach.

Please let it be interesting, Jonas thought to himself, knowing this was only the beginning. He knew the Amish believed in the "inspired message from God," and as a result, preachers weren't allowed to have notes with them. Some preachers were better than others as they combined storytelling, Bible-quoting, and admonishing the congregation into a 45- to 60-minute sermon.

"We have many young people here this morning in our midst," the preacher began. "But we have one less than we did a week ago. Today we have Enos Miller's body among us. But not Enos. No, not Enos. His life is gone from us, awaiting that judgment day—the judgment day we will all face.

"In Revelation 22 we read 'Blessed are those who wash their robes, that they may have the right to the tree of life and may go through the gates into the city. Outside are the dogs, those who practice magic arts, the sexually immoral, the murderers, the idolaters and everyone who loves and practices falsehood.'

"We will all face that judgment day. Will we be the sheep or the goats? Will the Lord say 'I never knew you' or will he say 'Well done, my good and faithful servant'?"

"That is the question our Enos faces. And it is the question for each of us."

The minister continued in the same vein for what seemed like a long time—Jonas guessed it to be about an hour. Then, almost abruptly, the minister quit talking, and another one stood up to announce the kneeling prayer. Everyone stood, turned, and knelt beside the wooden benches as the minister read a prayer from the prayer book. Jonas could hear the sounds of children, of adults, changing positions. He could feel the sweat running down his back under his white shirt and navy homemade jacket, and he could smell the perspiration of the people around him. By the time the long prayer was over, he ached to stand up and stretch his legs.

The congregation did stand for the next element of the service—a reading from the Bible. Then the second minister stood up to preach.

"My heart is heavy for the Miller family this morning," he began. "Today they bury a son, a brother, a grandson. Today they say good-bye to Enos. Today they lay him to rest among the others who have gone before us."

At the preacher's words, cries and sobs broke out among the listeners, and Jonas wished he could ignore the harshness, the dark stark reality. No, no, no!

Jonas tried to shut out much of the next hour. He refused to let his emotions go, and it was becoming more difficult as those around him wept. Finally the preacher stopped, and asked for comments and consent from the other ministers.

One by one, the seven other ministers responded to the sermon. Jonas found it easier to pay attention to those who were visiting from other communities—he didn't know them like he did the local preachers. Some brought a perspective he hadn't heard before.

After another kneeling prayer and a song, the three-hour service drew to a close. Then it was time for the entire congregation to file by the casket for a final viewing. When the pallbearers' turn came, Jonas told himself he wouldn't look—not really. He didn't want to remember Enos this way. He'd remember him laughing and joking—not lifeless and silent.

Jonas's resolve worked as he walked past the casket, seeing yet not absorbing the finality of the death before him. He was the last one out of the shed except for the family. As he walked out, several men closed the doors behind him. The family would now spend their last few moments with the body before the funeral caravan transported it to the cemetery.

While waiting for the family, Levi Petersheim pulled the funeral buggy up to the shed doors. The special hearse was drawn by Levi's matched pair of dark bay geldings. Any other time, Jonas's heart and eyes would have admired the horses, but now they blurred into the task at hand.

When the doors opened and the grieving family emerged, Levi went in to put the lid on the coffin for the final time. The pallbearers followed behind, slowly picked up the casket, carried it out of the shed, and slid it into the back of the funeral buggy. Levi got into the buggy, while the young men climbed into Fred Bontrager's surrey that he'd hitched up for Jonas. He handed Jonas the reins, and Jonas slapped them several times across the mare's back. They left the yard at a walk, but once on the road, Jonas set the mare in a steady trot toward the cemetery three miles away. They needed to be there ahead of the funeral procession.

Thirty minutes later, the pallbearers waiting at the cemetery could see the funeral procession approaching them. Jonas counted 60 buggies strung out down the paved road, and more were still coming. As the first ones began arriving, he turned his attention to the hearse buggy.

When everyone had arrived at the cemetery, the teenage pallbearers slid the pine coffin out of the hearse and carried it to the grave site. Since the only service the Amish desired from the funeral home was embalming, the customary tent, artificial turf, chairs and other "amenities" were missing. The boys set the coffin down on a simple wooden frame over the hole they'd dug the day before.

After a reading out of a traditional Amish book, a song, and a prayer out of a prayer book, the pallbearers attached ropes to the casket and slowly lowered it into the ground. Jonas told himself to concentrate on the mechanics of what he was doing, and not to think about anything else. It worked until the coffin was down, the ropes gathered up, and one of the ministers handed him a shovel.

Jonas scooped up some dirt from the pile beside the grave, and methodically threw it into the hole. The loud CLUNK! of dirt clods hitting the wooden coffin jarred the growing lump in his throat. He was throwing dirt on top of the body of his best friend, Enos! Enos was dead! Gone! Jonas's vision blurred. He handed the shovel to the person next to him, and then for the first time since the shooting, sobs shook his strong young shoulders.

Somewhere in the midst of the storm raging within him, Jonas heard his father's voice lead out in singing again, and the gathered people joining in. While some sang, others took turns shoveling. Head down low on his chest, Jonas couldn't watch. When he did look up, he wished he hadn't. It was just in time to see the last corner of the coffin being covered with dark black Kansas sod.

Chapter 15
Sue Ann

"When my grandma died, I just kept telling myself I'd see her again someday," Debbie said, chasing a fly off her hamburger. "It was still terribly hard to lose her, but I guess knowing that was sorta comforting."

Seated across from Debbie, eating lunch at the Schmidt picnic table, Jonas scooped some pork and beans up with a potato chip and slipped it into his mouth. His eyes gazed vacantly into the distance.

"Enos is probably in heaven now, riding his skateboard too fast on the golden streets," Debbie continued. "Can't you just see it?"

No, he couldn't. He didn't have any security at all about Enos's destiny after death. And he couldn't understand someone who thought she knew what happened to people after they died, not to mention skateboarding in heaven. Why would Debbie know more about Enos's fate than the Amish bishop and preachers? They studied their Bibles all the time. They knew what was in there. He looked at Debbie, then away again.

"We don't have to talk about it," she said. "It must still hurt a lot."

Hurt? Yeah, that was part of it, Jonas thought. It'd been a week since the funeral, and this was his first day back working for the Schmidts. He'd been helping the Millers with their farm and field work up until now. Yesterday he'd been working a field with a team of horses. Today he would be driving a huge John Deere tractor on Harlan's fields. The difference hit him like never before.

Other differences felt strange too. Debbie's approach to death, for one thing. She'd sent him a card after Enos died. Inside she'd written "Remember, God is like a big van, always ready to welcome another one of his people inside." Then she'd written more about how Jonas should talk to her youth leaders—that they could help him deal with these tough times. "God doesn't send bad things—he just promises to help us through them," she'd concluded, and then signed the card "All my love, and God's—Debbie."

As much as he liked Debbie, something wasn't feeling the same anymore. The talk about God he heard from her, and what he'd heard all his life and at the funeral—it was just so different. And getting a card signed "All my love, and God's"? Come on. Since when was God so loving and easy-to-get-along-with? And since when was Debbie giving him "all her love"?

"Shall we do something this Saturday evening?" Debbie's question brought Jonas back to the present.

"This Saturday? I probably have a baseball game."

"Okay, I'll come to the game and then we can go eat afterwards."

"Sure."

Enos's Mustang—the one he never returned to drive on the 4th of July—was gone when Jonas and his other teammates arrived at the ball diamond that Saturday evening. One of the guys had heard that Enos's father had given the keys to Sam, Sue Ann's ex-boyfriend, and told him to sell it. David Miller didn't want the money for it either—he'd donated it to an Amish family whose daughter had leukemia and, as a result, a lot of medical expenses. Jonas was glad the Mustang was gone—he didn't need the reminder of Enos.

Jonas had trouble concentrating on the game that night, and the fact that Enos was missing was only part of the problem. He knew he had to talk to Debbie. He'd done a lot of thinking since the shooting, and she needed to hear some of it. It wouldn't be easy.

"Hey, that was a great catch in the sixth inning!" Debbie enthused, wrapping her arm inside his as she and Jonas walked to her car after the game. "Where do you want to eat? I'm buying!"

❖ ❖ ❖

"It's just that I think you're getting more serious than I am," Jonas tried to explain as he and Debbie sat in her car, parked on a country road later that evening. "It seems like we're going steady or something. I'm not ready for that."

"I don't understand. What do I do that makes you feel like I'm too serious?"

Jonas didn't want to get into the details. He didn't want to talk about the card. He didn't want to say that part of his hesitancy was Debbie's style of religion, that it made him uncomfortable. He certainly didn't want to say that Enos's death had made him think twice about his life.

"It's hard to explain," he answered. "I've got a lot on my mind right now. It's just not the right time for me to have a serious dating relationship." He took her hand in his. "Please understand."

"I think I do," Debbie said quietly. "It's your Amish upbringing. You've been this way since Enos died."

Debbie paused, and when Jonas didn't respond, she continued.

"You're feeling really bad about what happened. What can I do to help you through this time?"

"Nothing," Jonas answered. "I have to work through this by myself. There's no way you can understand." You don't know how it feels to sit in the funeral of your best friend, he thought. You don't know what it's like to hear a preacher talk about judgment day, and asking you where you stand. You don't know what it's like to have your parents telling you that if you go astray, God will punish them forever.

Jonas and Debbie sat close for a long, painful silence, each lost in thought, searching for words. Finally Debbie spoke, her voice trembling, eyes glistening.

"So what you're needing, instead of a list of Amish pick-up lines, is a good break-up line?" Debbie's question caught Jonas completely off guard. He could see the deep disappointment in her eyes—he'd expected that. But the brave, half-smile on her lips? He managed a grin in return.

"I hadn't thought of it that way."

"How about 'I'm sorry, ma'am, but that Plymouth Horizon of yours is just too fast for me. I much prefer driving a runaway buggy.'"

Jonas laughed softly. "That'll work."

It was almost midnight, and time for Debbie to get home. Jonas knew the Amish young folks were having a party at their customary place along the river. He asked Debbie if she could drop him off there, and she agreed. When they got to the lane leading from the country road down to the river, Jonas said he could walk from there.

"We're still friends, right?" he said in the darkness to the girl beside him.

"Of course. Who else am I going to get to feed the calves with me?"

"Good. I like that." He opened his door and stepped out, then looked back. "Thanks for the ride, and for...for everything else." Leaning across the front seat toward Debbie, he kissed her lightly on the cheek. "See ya."

"See ya."

Without Enos, a lot of the life had gone out of the Amish young folks' party that night. When Jonas walked in, he saw groups of kids sitting around, playing cards, talking, drinking and eating. It was the quietest party he'd ever seen. Someone was wading in the river, and when he got closer, he recognized Sue

Ann. He stood on the edge of the muddy water, watching the solitary figure. Her head was down—she didn't seem to have noticed him.

"Hey," Jonas said by way of greeting as she came closer.

"Oh! It's you, Jonas! When did you get here?"

"Just a little bit ago. Debbie dropped me off."

"So how's Debbie these days?" Sue Ann walked out of the water and onto the sandy beach.

"I guess she's okay," Jonas paused, digging a hole in the sand with the toe of his Nike. "I told her tonight that she was getting more serious than I wanted to."

"Really? How come?"

"How come what?"

"Why did you all of a sudden think she's too serious? I thought you liked her a lot."

"I do. As a friend. But I guess maybe you were right. Remember when you said something about we were born Amish, and that's what we're meant to be? I've been thinking about that. Especially since Enos died."

The two started walking along the beach until the Coleman lanterns no longer illuminated their footsteps. It didn't really matter. The expansive Kansas night sky with its endless stars and three-quarter moon was light enough.

"Yeah, I know what you mean. Those preachers laid it on pretty heavy at the funeral, didn't they?" Sue Ann said.

"I guess that's part of it. I kept wondering, 'What if it'd been me?' You know?"

"I think we all thought that. And it could have been. Enos wasn't doing anything wrong. He didn't deserve to get killed."

"You don't think God was punishing him?"

"I'm not sure what I think about that, Jonas."

"Debbie says God doesn't send bad things, he just helps us through them."

"I don't know if God sends them or not, but it seems to me we sometimes need bad things to make us think about stuff."

"I guess that's what happened with me and Debbie. I got to thinking about life."

"So how did she take it—when you told her?"

"At first she didn't understand, and then—it was so strange. She was almost crying, and then she said, 'I guess what you need is an Amish break-up line rather than a pick-up line.'"

"What?"

"Oh it goes back to this list of Amish pick-up lines we made up at the New Year's Eve party. She was just making a joke, and saying I needed a break-up line instead."

"Oh. Do you remember some of the pick-up lines?"

"Not right offhand. They were pretty funny though."

Jonas and Sue Ann walked several miles that night, talking. When they got back to the party, many of the kids had crashed, rolled up in sleeping bags on the sand, on the backs of pickups, in cars and buggies.

"You bring something to sleep on?" Sue Ann queried.

"Not really."

"You can share mine," she indicated a blanket spread out under one of the few trees along the river.

"On one condition," Jonas said, looking at the blanket under a huge cottonwood. "We need to pull it out from under that tree. I want to see the stars."

"Sure. I didn't know you were such a stargazer."

"Gives me something to do 'til I fall asleep. You know what Debbie said? She said Enos is probably in heaven riding his skateboard too fast on the golden streets. Maybe we can see him."

Jonas looked at Sue Ann, wanting to see her reaction as well as hear it.

"What a strange thing to say."

"That's what I thought," Jonas paused, then laughed softly.

"But you know, it sounds like Enos!"

**Chapter
15**

The next day, Sunday, church was held at the David Miller home. Since everything had been cleaned up for the funeral, and the church wagon with its benches was still there, the Miller's offered to take their turn at church. That evening, the young folks gathered for the customary singing.

Ordinarily, the teenage girls would wear prim pastel dresses, belted at the waist, neatly cuffed at the short sleeves. Tonight, and for a month or so to follow, that light apparel would be replaced by black in memory of Enos. His female relatives would be wearing black for several months, too.

Jonas had known the girls would be in black, but the initial sight still surprised him, and sent a stab of pain through his being. He spotted Sue Ann among the group. She was listening to another one of the girls, her brown eyes intent and sincere. The combination of her high cheekbones, deeply tanned face, and dark hair pulled back under her covering brought another kind of gasp to his senses. If she wasn't one of the prettiest Amish girls he'd ever seen... Not to mention nice enough to spend half the night talking to, he grinned to himself.

The thought that came next almost made him chuckle out loud. Yes. Yes!

Working his way toward the group of girls, Jonas caught Sue Ann's eye. It was almost time to go inside for the singing. When she got close, Jonas touched her lightly on the arm and said, "I just remembered one of those Amish pick-up lines I told you about."

"Oh?"

"You wanna hear it?"

"Well, hurry up already, Jonas!" she laughed.

"Okay, this is it," Jonas stepped back just enough to scan Sue

Ann quickly from head to toe. "You're one hot babe," he paused, a broad grin spreading across his face. "We're not related, are we?"

"Jonas! You're embarrassing me!" Sue Ann covered her cheeks with her hands, but her dark eyes danced with pleasure.

Their eyes met and laughed silently, then Jonas and Sue Ann strolled side by side into the singing.

The End

Coming next:
Hitched
Book 2 ❖ Jonas Series

The Authors

Husband-and-wife authors Maynard Knepp and Carol Duerksen share their farm between Goessel and Hillsboro, Kansas, with exchange students and a variety of animals. Maynard grew up Amish near Yoder, Kansas, and provided the inspiration and information for this book. He manages a hog facility near Hutchinson.

Carol is a full-time freelance writer. She coedits *With*, a Christian youth magazine, and writes Sunday school curriculum, among other projects. Maynard and Carol are active members of the Tabor Mennonite Church.

The Illustrator

Susan Bartel has illustrated several books and many magazine stories. She lives with her husband and two children at Rocky Mountain Mennonite Camp near Divide, Colorado.

OTHER BOOKS FROM

WILLOWSPRING DOWNS

JONAS SERIES

The Jonas Series was the brainchild of Maynard Knepp, a popular speaker on the Amish culture who grew up in an Amish family in central Kansas. Knepp and his wife Carol Duerksen, a freelance writer, collaborated to produce their first book, *Runaway Buggy*, released in October, 1995. The resounding success of that book encouraged them to continue, and the series grew to four books within 18 months. The books portray the Amish as real people who face many of the same decisions, joys and sorrows as everyone else, as well as those that are unique to their culture and tradition. Written in an easy-to-read style that appeals to a wide range of ages and diverse reader base — from elementary age children to folks in their 90s, from dairy farmers to PhDs — fans of the Jonas Series are calling it captivating, intriguing, can't-put-it-down reading.

RUNAWAY BUGGY

This book sweeps the reader into the world of an Amish youth trying to find his way "home." Not only does *Runaway Buggy* pull back a curtain to more clearly see a group of people, but it intimately reveals the heart of one of their sons struggling to become a young man all his own.

HITCHED

With *Hitched*, the second installment in the Jonas Series, the reader struggles with Jonas as he searches for the meaning of Christianity and tradition, and feels his bewilderment as he recognizes that just as there are Christians who are not Amish, there are Amish who are not Christians.

PREACHER

Book Three in the Jonas Series finds Jonas Bontrager the owner of a racehorse named Preacher, and facing dilemmas that only his faith can explain, and only his faith can help him endure.

BECCA

The fourth book in the Jonas Series invites readers to see the world through the eyes of Jonas Bontrager's 16-year-old daughter Becca, as she asks the same questions her father did, but in her own fresh and surprising ways.

Slickfester Dude Tells Bedtime Stories
Life Lessons from our Animal Friends

by Carol Duerksen (& Slickfester Dude)

WillowSpring Downs is not only a publishing company — it's also a 120-acre piece of paradise in central Kansas that's home to a wide assortment of animals. Slickfester Dude, a black cat with three legs that work and one that doesn't, is one of those special animals. In a unique book that only a very observant cat could write, Slickfester Dude tells Carol a bedtime story every night — a story of life among the animals and what it can mean for everyone's daily life. This book will delight people from elementary age and up because the short stories are told in words that both children and adults can understand and take to heart. Along with strong, sensitive black and white story illustrations, the book includes Slickfester Dude's Photo Album of his people and animal friends at WillowSpring Downs.

O R D E R   F O R M

Jonas Series: *($9.95 each* **OR** *2 or more, any title mix, $10 each, we pay shipping.)*

_____ copy/copies of *Runaway Buggy*

_____ copy/copies of *Hitched*

_____ copy/copies of *Preacher*

_____ copy/copies of *Becca*

_____ Jonas Series—all 4 books, $36.50

> For more information or to be added to our mailing list, call or fax us on our toll-free number
>
> **1-888-551-0973**

Skye Series:

_____ copy/copies of *Twins* @ $9.95 each

Other:

_____ copy/copies of *Slickfester Dude Tells Bedtime Stories* @ $9.95 each

Name _____

Address _____

City _____ State _____

Zip _____ Phone # _____

_____ Book(s) at $9.95 = Total $ _____

Add $3 postage/handling if only one copy _____

SPECIAL PRICE = Buy 2 or more, pay $10 each and we'll pay the shipping.

Total enclosed $ _____

Make checks payable to WillowSpring Downs and mail, along with this order form, to the following address:

**WillowSpring Downs
Route 2, Box 31
Hillsboro, KS 67063-9600**